MW01257928

REMEMBERING THE COWBOY

A CONTEMPORARY CHRISTIAN ROMANCE

BLACKWATER RANCH
BOOK ONE

MANDI BLAKE

CONTENTS

Remembering the Cowboy
Blackwater Ranch Book One
By Mandi Blake

Copyright © 2020 Mandi Blake
All Rights Reserved

No part of this book may be used or reproduced in any manner whatsoever without written permission, except in the case of brief quotations embedded in critical articles and reviews. The unauthorized reproduction or distribution of this copyrighted work is illegal. No part of this book may be scanned, uploaded or distributed via the Internet or any other means, electronic or print, without the author's permission.

This book is a work of fiction. The names, characters, places, and incidents are products of the writer's imagination or have been used fictitiously and are not to be construed as real. Any resemblance to persons, living or dead, actual events, locale or organizations is entirely coincidental. The author does not have any control over and does not assume any responsibility for third-party websites or their content.

Published in the United States of America
Cover Designer: Amanda Walker PA & Design Services
Editor: Editing Done Write
Ebook ISBN: 978-1-7344302-4-0
Paperback ISBN: 978-1-7344302-5-7

CHAPTER 1
CAMILLE

Camille Vanderbilt was back in Wyoming on a mission: find Noah Harding.

She tapped her heel against the floorboard of her Camry as she drove. The closer she got to Blackwater, the closer she got to the place that would always be her home. She'd stayed away far too long this time, and she wasn't leaving again without talking to the man who used to be her best friend.

Camille arched her back. The drive from Portland was long, but she'd take a road trip over flying any day. Those landing strips were way too short for her taste. Safer to keep her feet on the ground.

Speaking of where her feet belonged, a snow-covered field dominated the landscape to her left, and she knew it would be a sprawling sea of green in summer. The forest to her right was a maze of brown trunks and branches shrouded in white.

A summer visit was definitely in order. She itched to feel the grass beneath her feet. The snow would be crunchy and frigid right now, but that was home. To love Wyoming, you had to endure the frigid winters to get to the perfect summers.

Camille always got antsy on the drive home. Eager to be back in the valley she loved, she'd gotten up and ready before dawn. The sun coming up over the Grand Tetons was a sight everyone should see at least once in their life. When she found herself on the western side of the iconic range, she took the chance to soak up the beautiful sight.

Her favorite tumbler, the one with the purple owl that read, "I don't give a hoot," kept her supplied with coffee. Rolling the window down half an inch, she breathed in the brisk air that filled her senses with the pine and mountains of home. The wind picked up her long chocolate-brown hair and twirled it into knots, but she didn't care. There wasn't a place on God's green earth that was better than Blackwater. She might live in the city now, but she was a country girl at heart.

A loud ring filled her car, startling her just as a robotic booming voice said, "Incoming call from Jenny Morris."

Camille jammed the button on her steering wheel to accept the call and stop the yelling. She needed to figure out how to adjust the volume on her Bluetooth. Apparently, turning the volume dial wasn't the answer. That would be too easy.

"Hey, Jen. Guess where I am," Camille answered with her usual pep.

"You'd better be close. I can't wait to see you!" Jenny was Camille's cousin, but they'd always been friends above all. They'd even been roommates in college.

"I'm only a few miles out. I have some things to take care of before I meet you and Mom at The Basket Case for lunch." This wasn't the first time Camille had tried to track down Noah Harding, and she wasn't giving up this time.

Jenny huffed. "Let me guess. It has something to do with Noah."

Camille's voice rose in volume and pitch. "Well, he couldn't have just disappeared, Jen!" Although, Camille sometimes thought he had. It'd been six years since she'd seen him, and she'd been back in Blackwater for holidays a dozen times since then with no sight or smell of him.

"He's here. He just doesn't want to be found."

That answer didn't satisfy Camille Vanderbilt. "Ready or not, here I come," she taunted.

Jenny sighed. "I'm sure he has his reasons. We both know he wouldn't be avoiding you if there wasn't a *really* good reason. That man always thought you hung the moon."

Camille frowned. She hated frowning. It felt

wrong. "If he did, he wouldn't be playing hide-and-seek with me."

Oh, she'd find Noah this time. She could feel it. Someone had to have an idea about where her best friend was hiding out.

Ex-best friend, she reminded herself. Noah wasn't her friend anymore.

Jenny's voice now held a tone of worry. "I hope you find him. You know I do. I just hope you find what you're looking for and not something worse."

"What does that mean?" Camille asked. "Stop being cryptic."

"I'm not. I just care about you. I don't know why he cut things off, but whatever it is, I don't think it can be good."

Camille had spent too much time wondering the same thing. She'd once felt certain that nothing could keep Noah from her. Since things changed six years ago, she hadn't stopped wondering what his reason could be. He'd stopped answering her phone calls and texts without warning.

"I'll see you later. Don't worry about me. I'm made of more spice than sugar."

Jenny's upbeat tone was back. "I love you, Millie."

"Love you too."

Camille disconnected the call and sucked in a deep breath. She could be tough. Whatever she found out about Noah, she could handle it.

She didn't know if she'd thump him in the forehead or kiss him when she found him, but she wasn't leaving this time until she had a heart-to-heart with the one who broke hers.

How dare he ghost her! They'd been best friends since middle school, and when things had *finally* turned into something more with him, he'd bailed! Sure, she'd been moving off to college, but she'd thought they were stronger than distance. They'd only talked about it a million times.

She relived that awful day over and over in her mind. How could she ever forget it? How could she get past it?

How could he have broken up with her? No, he hadn't even given her that much closure. This was exactly what she'd hoped to avoid by staying "friends" instead of giving in to the "more" they both wanted to be all throughout high school. She hadn't wanted to lose him—her best friend.

Now look what happened. She'd lived a blissful existence for a single week during the summer after high school graduation just to watch it crash and burn.

Camille had promised her younger self she wouldn't be one of those vapid women who couldn't think of anything except a man, but no one had warned her about Noah Harding and unrequited love.

Sure, she'd dated men in college and after, but it

was hard not to compare when she'd known a love like the one she and Noah had shared.

Yep, she decided to thump him really hard between the eyes when she found him. Maybe she'd even kick him in the shin for good measure. She loved him with all her heart, but she'd been mad at him for years, and her anger needed an outlet.

Waylon Jennings crooned the slow words of "Amanda" on the golden oldies station Camille listened to every time she visited home. If fate should have made Amanda a gentleman's wife, Camille wanted to put in her bid for a rancher's wife. The song was like a memory. It was all she had left—memories.

She wasn't even sure Noah was still working on his family ranch. He'd always wanted to be a fire-fighter. During her last visit home, she'd stopped by the ranch and tried to coax some information from his mama, but she was tight-lipped, keeping the subject always on Camille.

She wouldn't be deterred this time. She was going to march right up to Anita Harding's doorstep, and she wasn't leaving until she had some answers. Camille might even get an oatmeal raisin cookie if she was lucky.

She had to have hope. Maybe the Lord was making her wait for a reason. She'd have to trust it was a good one.

She passed a small, white church and wondered

if she'd see him at the service. Did he even go to the same church anymore? There weren't that many options for community worship on this side of town.

Her parents had attended somewhere else closer to the town of Cody, but she'd always gone to services with Noah. Camille and Noah had been inseparable once. Now, everything just reminded her of him—a song they'd danced to, his favorite shade of nail polish she wore, horses grazing in a field.

And Colorado. Always Colorado.

They'd made a quirky pair back then. He drew the lines and she crossed them. Of course, everyone in town had assumed the opposite. Noah was tall, dark, and handsome with broad shoulders that assured him a few suspicious side glances from the townsfolk.

On the other hand, Camille was a Vanderbilt and could do no wrong. She supposed people overlooked her antics, since her father and his ancestors built half the town.

He wasn't her biological father. Her dad died just a few weeks after her eighth birthday, and by the time Camille was ten years old, her mom had married Nathan Vanderbilt, who had adopted her soon after. Camille had been happy at the time. Her stepdad accepted her wholeheartedly and consid- ered her one of the elite Vanderbilts. Her innocent heart hadn't understood the full weight of the name. Camille often wondered if Nathan would have been so welcoming of her if she'd refused to take his last name.

Camille was only ten miles from home when another call rang through the car's Bluetooth. Good grief, it was loud. It was as if her mother had a tracker on her.

She rolled the window up and answered. "Hey, Mom. Did you hear me coming?"

Bonnie Vanderbilt had a heart of gold, but she'd always called Camille her greatest treasure. "Just checking on you. I assumed you'd get an early start on your drive."

Camille had driven halfway home yesterday and stopped in Idaho for the night. "I left before dawn. I'll be there in a few hours. I have some things I need to do in town first."

"How's the drive? Are you being cautious?"

Camille fought to contain her grin. Being away from Noah hadn't been *all* bad these years. She'd learned to drive at least. There'd been no reason to learn when Noah drove her everywhere she wanted to go in his old pickup truck. She might have started her car a handful of times in those years.

She hadn't gotten her license until she was eighteen when Nathan had laid down the law. He assured her she'd need to drive when she moved away to Oregon for law school. During college, her cousin and roommate, Jenny, helped her navigate the rules of the road.

"This isn't my first rodeo, Mom. I drive home at least once a year."

"Okay, sweetie. Are you sure everything is going to be okay at work if you take this much time off?"

Of course, her parents would always worry about her job above all else. Nathan had secured her position at Parker and Lions long before she'd attained her law license. Appearances were everything to the Vanderbilts.

"They'll survive."

Camille really didn't care how the firm held up in her absence. She was tired of corporate sticks barking orders at her as if she were nothing more than the dirt beneath their wingtip shoes.

If she'd followed her heart and gone into family law, then she would care. Those were real people who needed help. Not the corporate lackeys she worked for. Camille wanted to make a difference in people's lives, but her current job left her feeling sick and hollow.

"Well, if you're sure it's all right. We don't want you upsetting the higher-ups."

"I know, Mom." The reply was curt but not disrespectful.

"Jenny said she'd meet us at the restaurant at eleven. After lunch, we can walk to some of the boutique shops in town."

Tomorrow was Jenny's birthday and the main reason for Camille's trip home. Christmas was next weekend, and the timing had prompted her to extend her stay in Wyoming for a full two weeks. She hadn't been home for more than a weekend in years. Not since before she started the soul-sucking job at Parker and Lions.

"Sounds perfect. I miss y'all like crazy."

Camille's mother's voice was sweet as always. "I know you do, dear. I'm so glad you had Jenny with you during college out on the coast. I worried about you..."

Her mother's sentence trailed off. They both knew her concern arose from Camille's lack of friends. Camille had attached herself to two people throughout middle school and high school—Noah and Jenny. They were all she ever needed, but Camille's mother could never understand her aversion to networking.

"I held up fine." Camille's words held her usual pep and assurance, but they felt hollow as they left her lips. She didn't have one friend she could name in Portland since Jenny left, and she'd been living there for years.

"I know, sweetie. Just get on home, and we'll—"

A bulking form dove from the tree line to Camille's right, and her chest constricted just as the deer crashed into the passenger side of her car, sending glass flying. Camille tensed from the impact and her foot slid from the accelerator as her shoulders lifted to her ears. She grabbed for the wheel, but the car was moving erratically, and she couldn't tell which way was straight.

Before she could right her vehicle, an oncoming truck crashed into her car on the passenger side and Camille's world went black.

CHAPTER 2
NOAH

Noah Harding sucked in deep breaths through his nose as he ran. Sweat poured down his face and drenched his navy-blue Blackwater Fire Department T-shirt.

Jameson panted through his words as he ran beside Noah. "I picked up the fence posts yesterday. We need to mend the south fence on the field by the back entrance. Or should we fix the one that's down by Bluestone Creek?"

"We can do both," Lucas quipped from Noah's other side.

"I'm volunteering on Monday, but I can help you finish up whatever's left on Tuesday," Noah added.

Noah liked Jameson, but Lucas didn't have any love for the guy. Lucas was a Harding, so working the ranch was expected of him, but their dad hired Jameson a couple of years ago. Jameson was a perfectionist and a little obsessive, and those traits didn't mesh well with Lucas's fun-loving nature.

"What about the broken tines on the baler?" Jameson asked through heaving breaths pushed out by the force of his run.

Lucas stumbled and grunted. "I forgot about that."

Noah panted. "Asher and Micah can take care of that."

Lucas shook his head at Noah. "I don't envy Ash. Micah will micromanage the installation to death." Micah was their eldest brother and he co-managed Blackwater Ranch next to their father.

"I can help with that too," Jameson panted.

Lucas rolled his eyes. "Of course, you can."

Jameson craned his neck to check out Lucas's stats on the treadmill. "You're comin' up short, Lucas. You been spending' too much time chattin' up the horses?"

Lucas's face turned a deep shade of red as he picked up the pace and ignored Jameson. Lucas was the horse expert at Blackwater Ranch, but he worked all parts of the ranch just like the rest of them. The competition between Lucas and Jameson had raged on since high school sports. These days, they competed to see who the hardest worker at the ranch was, both seeking the highest approval from Silas Harding, Noah and Lucas's dad.

How had Noah gotten stuck running on the

treadmill between these two? Jameson was asking for trouble, and Noah knew Lucas was about to tell Jameson to hit the road.

Of all the Hardings, Noah probably spoke the least. If he had something worth saying, he'd say it. Otherwise, he kept to himself. Listening was his strong suit.

"I got a date Friday night," Jameson bragged.

Lucas turned his attention toward Jameson. "She a guest at the Chambers Dude Ranch?" Jameson also worked part time at the dude ranch nearby, and the brothers joked that he always had a date with the out-of-towners.

"Yeah, she's a hairdresser in Chicago visiting with her folks."

Lucas gave an exasperated huff and turned his attention back to the treadmill screen.

Noah hadn't had a serious date in... well, ever. Nothing to write home about since Camille moved off to Portland.

Camille. Everything reminded him of Camille Vanderbilt and how he hadn't seen her gorgeous face in years.

That's one reason why he hated listening to Jameson talk about his dates. None of the women stuck around, but it didn't seem to bother him that the happiness was fleeting.

Noah had a perfect relationship once. It lasted all of sixty seconds before it blew up in his face.

That's what he got for thinking he could have the most unattainable woman in town.

Hearing Jameson talk about the women he dated just reminded Noah that Camille was gone, and no one had come close to filling that void since she'd left.

Noah turned to his right to find Lucas's face lit up in a victorious smile. "I'm holding the lead. Get ready to wash my dirty socks, boys."

Noah was an exceptional runner, and so was Jameson, but Lucas was a machine. With his tall, lean build, he put the Energizer Bunny to shame.

Arms pumping through the home stretch, Jameson grumbled something about putting in an extra workout this week that had Noah stumbling into a laugh. Jameson and Lucas could fight it out for all Noah cared.

The tones dropped, sounding the alarm for a call before anyone reached the finish line. Jameson punched his power-off button first.

Lucas yelled, "No! I was winning."

"Suit up, boys," Jameson barked over his shoulder as he tore out of the room ahead of them both.

Noah turned off his machine and followed Jameson out the door, drying his sweat with a towel.

Lucas bounced up behind him, adrenaline pumping from the run and the call. "Show time!"

Noah clapped a heavy hand on Lucas's back and

got to work. Each call was like a dog whistle to Noah. Every moment after that warning demanded his full attention. After years of training and action, getting ready for a call was a matter of muscle memory. Their crew was a machine, trained to perfection.

Noah hopped into the ambulance beside Jameson, his partner EMT, and they were off to save some lives. He refused to entertain the thought of anything except saving.

The police had already blocked off the road when they arrived. The two-car collision—a Camry and an F-150—made the way completely impassible to oncoming traffic. Noah stepped up to the mangled vehicles. Lucas was standing beside the open driver's door of the Camry.

"Noah! Get over here!"

Noah grabbed the medical bag and ran to help. Lucas's call had sent a chill down Noah's spine.

He ran to the car and peered in the window. Through a spider web crack in the glass, he could see long dark hair framing a bloody face.

Camille's face.

"No. No!" Noah was around the door in an instant, shoving past Lucas to get to her.

Noah stabilized her neck as he heard Lucas telling Jameson to check on the other driver. Noah leaned in and closed his eyes to detect a breath and pressed his fingers to her throat. A faint but rhythmic pulse tickled his fingertips. She was unconscious but alive.

"Let's get her out," Noah barked as Lucas stepped in beside him, ready to carefully extract her from the vehicle.

Lucas lifted her core and lower body while Noah had her upper body and neck stabilized.

Jameson was back from checking on the other driver and had the longboard ready. Noah and Lucas stepped backwards and turned Camille to the direction of the board.

Jameson silently helped Noah secure her in place. Noah's assessing gaze traveled from her head to her feet. She was the same in all the ways he remembered, but she was different in subtle ways that gripped his heart. Her head wound was still bleeding, and they worked together to bandage it. Noah's hands were shaking as he tore the tape to secure the gauze. The wound would need to be closed at the hospital.

Noah couldn't see any other major bleeding, but that didn't mean the unseen killer wasn't working its death on her insides. Jameson was prepping an IV, and Noah took the moment to school his panic. The shaking in his hands had subsided by the time Jameson passed him the IV, and Noah administered it flawlessly. His years of training had all been leading up to this moment.

"Let's get her in." Noah nodded at Jameson as they lifted her into the ambulance.

Lucas clapped a hand on Noah's shoulder before he stepped into the ambulance. "Hey."

Noah turned to his brother and swallowed the lump in his throat. He couldn't speak if his life depended on it.

Lucas's face was serious and sure. He was the only one here who knew about Noah's past with Camille Vanderbilt. He just didn't know the whole story—the ending. Only their brother, Micah, knew the reason for the separation, and it was only because he was the manager of Blackwater Ranch.

Lucas nodded. "You got this."

Noah nodded and stepped into the ambulance with Camille. He closed the doors, and Jameson started their course for the hospital.

Alone with Camille, Noah made the necessary assessments. He listened to her lung sounds and heard the beat of her heart. Closing his eyes, he took a deep breath and prayed they'd both have the strength to get through this—with minimal scars.

He turned to her, determined to find something that would bring her back to him. He was living his worst nightmare, and he couldn't stand it any longer. He checked every lifesaving measure he could think of, while whispering a prayer under his breath.

Frantically, he checked the IV and her lung

sounds again. Nothing was pulling her back to consciousness, and he panicked. "Camille! Don't leave me! Come back to me!"

Failing wasn't an option. This was Camille. His Camille. She was back. He could touch her. He'd never wanted to be away from her in the first place. She was real, and he couldn't lose her.

Not again.

Noah watched as Camille's eyes fluttered open, and he scrambled to her. "Camille! I'm here. Come back to me."

Her face was a mask of confusion, but her voice was angelic. "What happened?"

"You were in a wreck. It's okay now." Noah trailed his fingers over her temple and the bandage. The strands of her hair were a shade darker around the wound where it was matted together by her blood.

Her eyes narrowed then shifted from him. "What happened?"

It was common for head wounds to cause confusion. He just needed to keep her stable. "You were in a wreck. You're going to be all right." He checked her vitals again and breathed a sigh of relief as Jameson turned into the drive of Cody Memorial Hospital. "We're almost there. Hang on."

Camille's bright-green eyes drifted closed, and she fell back into unconsciousness.

"No!" Noah screamed, as Jameson parked the

ambulance and ran to open the doors. It was a blessing she'd regained consciousness, and Noah wasn't ready to let go of his hope just yet.

Jameson helped Noah get her out of the ambulance and transfer her to the nurse's care. Jameson started the paperwork, while Noah waited for the doctor who would clear her to be removed from the longboard.

Noah studied Camille's face with a calmness he didn't feel. His insides were roiling. Seeing her almost lifeless had his chest constricting to the point of pain.

"Excuse me! Is that my daughter?"

Noah turned. He'd know that voice anywhere. Bonnie Vanderbilt shuffled up to him in the hallway, holding the strap of her purse as it bounced against her hip.

A petite nurse in pink scrubs stuck her arm out to Bonnie. "Excuse me, ma'am. Let us have some space."

"Noah?" Mrs. Vanderbilt asked as she reached for his hand.

Grasping her delicate fingers in his calloused grip, Noah squeezed. "It's me. She's gonna be fine. I'll make sure of it."

"Oh, you don't know how glad I am to see a friendly face." Bonnie wrapped her arms around his neck and squeezed.

It was strangely comforting to see Camille's

mom. He'd always loved Mrs. Vanderbilt like an extension of his family, and she'd never treated him with the disdain his social status required from the town's elite.

The doctor arrived as Camille was admitted into a room. Noah didn't want to leave her side, but Mrs. Vanderbilt held tight to his hand, and he knew she needed his assurance that her only daughter would make it through this.

Tears ran down Mrs. Vanderbilt's cheeks. She was young enough that time hadn't etched her face in wrinkles, but old enough to know that life wasn't always fair. Her first husband had died when Camille was only eight years old.

Noah clasped Mrs. Vanderbilt's hand in both of his. "Listen. I'll get a report in a second, and we'll know more. She gained consciousness for a few seconds, so that's grounds for hope."

Mrs. Vanderbilt nodded and chewed her bottom lip. "Did you pray, son?" Her words were broken and tired.

"I did," Noah confirmed.

"Bonnie." The gruff voice pierced the circle of hope they'd created and sent a lick of fire up Noah's spine.

Noah hadn't been sure this day could get any worse, but he was terribly mistaken as he lifted his chin to face Nathan Vanderbilt.

CHAPTER 3
NOAH

Noah squared his shoulders toward Camille's stepdad. Their last meeting had kicked off the worst period of Noah's life—the years he'd been forced to spend without Camille. Nathan Vanderbilt might hold all the cards, but Noah would never cower to another man. With as much calm as he could muster, Noah extended his hand in greeting. "Mr. Vanderbilt."

Nathan's gaze hadn't left Noah's, but his fist remained clenched at his side. A scowl painted the older man's face, but it was subtle. A Vanderbilt never truly showed his temper.

Bonnie released Noah's other hand and ran to her husband. "Oh, Nathan." She sobbed onto his chest. "She's in there, and she looked—"

"Yes," Nathan interrupted his wife. He spoke to her, but his focus was still trained on Noah. "Why don't you have a seat in the waiting room? I'll be right there."

Bonnie wasn't a pushover, but she liked to keep the peace, and she wasn't oblivious to the tension between her husband and Noah.

He retracted his waiting hand and crossed his arms over his chest.

Nathan gave Noah an appraising glance. "You again."

"Always me, sir," he retorted.

"The terms of our last meeting still stand."

Noah focused on slowing his breathing. His nostrils flared in protest. "Are we really still doing this?"

"A man is only as good as his word, and you gave yours," Nathan reminded Noah.

Forcing the anger down into the pit of his stomach, Noah countered, "A real man doesn't control his daughter's life through threats."

Nathan stepped closer. They both knew the game, and Noah had everything to lose.

"Listen closely," Nathan demanded. He was a few inches shorter than Noah, but it didn't seem to bother the older man. "No matter how old she gets, she'll always be too good for you."

No argument there, but it didn't mean he was ready to lie down and let the woman he loved get away... again.

"You can't do this."

"I can, and I will," Nathan promised.

Nathan lived in a world of black and white. You were rich and influential, or you were common and unworthy. Noah fell into the latter category, and the idea of Noah standing proud beside a Vanderbilt was the epitome of a disaster in Nathan's eyes. The Vanderbilts were the most powerful family in the area, and Nathan was the most ruthless.

Noah came from a family of ranchers. His family had owned and operated Blackwater Ranch for five generations. It was everything to his parents. If Noah was honest, it meant the world to him too.

A rancher couldn't give Camille the life she was accustomed to. Especially since Blackwater Ranch had spent the better part of Noah's childhood and teen years recovering from a massive fire that had almost destroyed their family business.

Nathan had his ear in everyone's business and knew exactly how the ranch was doing at all times. It wasn't enough for his daughter.

Noah kept his eyes on Nathan as red tinged the edges of his vision. Noah knew he'd never be more than a rancher's son or a firefighter, but Camille had always looked at him as if he'd hung the moon. That's all that mattered. She hadn't cared about his lack of money. She loved him. Why couldn't Nathan see that?

No, he'd never be one of those corporate puppets the Vanderbilts associated with, but he didn't care.

All he cared about was Camille, and her wellbeing was hanging in the balance as he stood here reliving the same argument with her stepdad.

He placed his hand on the door to Camille's room. "I'm going to check on Camille."

"No, you're not."

He took a deep breath through his nose and counted to three. It took everything he had not to throttle the old man.

Nathan whispered, "You stay away from her. I'll be telling the administration that you're not to have access to her room."

Noah stepped away before he did something he'd regret. He'd never been a violent person, but no one had ever stolen as much from him as Nathan Vanderbilt.

Noah found Jameson filling out forms in the EMS room with his feet propped on a nearby chair. He sat up straighter when he heard Noah enter in a huff.

"Hey, what's with all the tension? You know that woman?" Jameson asked.

Noah ran his hands through his hair and paced. "Yeah. I need to make a phone call."

He dialed Jenny's old number and prayed it hadn't changed. It'd been years since he'd talked to Camille's cousin.

Jenny's tone was cautious as she answered. "Hello?"

"Hey, Jen. It's Noah Harding. Camille's been in an accident. She's at Cody Memorial Hospital. Did they tell you?"

"No!" Jenny frantically spat. "I'm supposed to meet her and Bonnie in a little bit to go shopping. Is she okay?"

"Um, I'm not sure. The scene looked like there was a deer and another truck involved. She's in and out of consciousness, but I've been denied access to her room."

"Why are you there? How did you know about it? Why didn't anyone call me?" Jenny's pitch rose with each rapid-fire question.

"I'm an EMT. I was called to the scene. I'm sure Bonnie's been a little distracted since it happened." Noah scraped his hand through his hair. "Listen, can you come down here? I want to know how she's doing, but they won't let me see her." He could hear shuffling on the other end of the call.

"Why won't they let you in?" Jenny asked.

"Why do you think? Nathan doesn't like me, and he's on a power trip."

"Some things never change," Jenny mumbled. "I'm on my way."

Noah disconnected the call and squeezed the phone before sitting down hard in the chair beside Jameson.

"Um," Jameson began cautiously. "I know you're

not very keen on sharing, but any chance you want to fill me in on this one? You seem frazzled."

Noah tapped his fingers on the table where his arm rested. He had to think of a way around Nathan. "I don't want to talk about it."

"Of course not." Jameson sat back with a sarcastic grin. "I don't know why I asked."

"Sorry. I'm just in over my head here." Noah rubbed his jaw and stood again. He had way too much energy to sit here in this room. "It's someone I used to know. We were friends in high school."

Jameson nodded and asked, "How's she doing?"

Noah threw his hands in the air. "I don't know! Her stepdad won't let me near her."

"Why?"

Noah turned to Jameson. He didn't discuss his past with anyone. Lucas knew parts of it, but they never talked about it. "She's a Vanderbilt. Nathan Vanderbilt is her stepdad."

Jameson's eyes grew wide. "Um, yeah. Now I get it. Sheesh. That's... rotten luck."

Everyone in town knew Nathan Vanderbilt. His reputation preceded him, and the smart folks kept their distance.

"I don't know what to tell you." Jameson rubbed his forehead. If Noah's opinionated friend was at a loss for words, he was in trouble.

"Yeah, I haven't known the answer for about a

decade. Join the club." Noah sat down again and tapped his knuckle against the table.

"I'm done here. You coming?" Jameson asked as he stood.

Noah checked his phone again. "Nah, I'll wait a bit and see if Jenny can give me an update."

"I'll send Lucas back to get you when you're ready."

Noah sat alone in the room and prayed. He felt helpless, and the least he could do was ask for help.

A few minutes later, his phone buzzed. It was Jenny.

"Hey, where are you?" she asked in greeting.

"I'll meet you at the information desk." He was already walking, eager for an update on Camille.

When Jenny rounded the corner, Noah noticed that she looked much the same as she had before moving off to Portland with Camille for college. Jenny's sandy blonde hair was straight and just touched her shoulders—a few inches shorter than when they were young. A single crease fell between her brows, a sign of her worry. Jenny had always been the cautious rule follower—a nice compliment to Camille's impulsive free spirit.

"Hey, how is she?" he asked abruptly.

Jenny's jaw was set as she shook her head. "Still unconscious. They're monitoring everything, but we don't know much."

Noah hung his head in his hands to gather a

breath before facing her again. "Did they say I could see her?" It was a long shot, but he had to try.

Jenny placed a comforting hand on his arm. "I'm sorry, Noah. Emotions are high in there, and I know more than anyone how much you want to see her. I just don't think it's a good idea. Nathan won't back down right now." She slowly lifted her shoulder in defeat. "I think you should go."

Noah swallowed the lump in his throat and hung his head. "Will you keep me updated?"

"I will. I wish I could help," Jenny whispered.

Noah bit the inside of his cheek and nodded. "Okay. I'll just... wait to hear from you."

Jenny let her hand slip from his arm. Her green eyes, so much like Camille's, gave him one last glance full of pity before turning away.

He texted Lucas for a ride and made his way outside to wait. The air was frigid, but Noah was numb. The only thing he felt was the grip in his chest.

Pinching the bridge of his nose, he prayed for answers. How was he going to see Camille again?

CHAPTER 4
CAMILLE

Camille slowly opened her eyes and turned her head. Everything hurt.

"Sweetie? Sweetie, I'm here." Someone stood, hanging over her, assessing her with wide eyes.

Confusion filled her head, and it took a moment for the recognition to settle in place before she said, "Mom?"

Her mind was blank. She just stared—at her mother, at the walls. It hurt to turn her head much, but she didn't really care.

Her mother rattled on, calling for a nurse, asking for the doctor.

Camille just stared, not sure what to think because it was hard to focus long enough to think about any one thing. Thoughts shot around in her head, vying for her attention, but darting away too fast to catch. It was exhausting.

Nurses came to assess her, followed by a doctor. Finally, Camille asked, "What happened?"

A nurse in pink scrubs with a copper pixie cut answered, "You were in a wreck. You've been in a coma for two days."

The information didn't register. The pain over-powered everything else. "My head."

"Do you need something for the pain?" the pixie nurse asked.

"Yeah." Camille closed her eyes and gave in to the darkness.

The next time Camille opened her eyes, a man was sitting in the chair beside her bed. His elbow was propped on the arm of the chair and his cheek rested in his hand. His eyes were closed in a deep sleep. His salt-and-pepper hair was cut neat, and she had a vague sense of familiarity.

The notion that she *should* know him was the only thing keeping her calm. She wasn't sure where she was or why she was here. Tubes and bandages were everywhere. It was a hospital, but she didn't know why she would be here.

Her mother stepped into the room with a disposable coffee cup in hand. When she realized Camille was awake, she shoved the man's shoulder. "Nathan, get up. She's awake."

"Mom? What happened?"

Pushing her cup into Nathan's hands, her mother sat on the side of Camille's bed. "You were in an accident. The doctors say you're doing okay. Sleep is good for you, so just keep resting."

Her mom hadn't let go of Camille's hand since sitting on the bed. While her mother cooed about sleep and rest, Camille cast a glance at the man her mother had called Nathan.

"Come talk to her. They said we should talk." Her mother waved him over.

"Hey, sweetie. How's your head?" he asked with genuine concern.

Camille wasn't sure of anything except the pain. She'd never felt so... blank. "What happened?"

Her mother's eyes went glassy, and she squeezed Camille's hand. "You were in a wreck. You're going to be all right," her mother replied slowly.

Suddenly, Camille had a memory of a dark-haired man surrounded by a bright light, but his face was cast in shadow. She could hear his screams.

"Camille! Don't leave me!"

Startled out of the memory, Camille's breathing quickened. She remembered his panic so vividly. "Where is he?"

Her mother shook her head. "Where is who?"

"The man. The man in the... light."

It didn't make sense to her when she said the words aloud, but there had been a man. She knew it.

She was confused, and the pounding in her head was demanding attention. She placed a hand on her temple as if she could keep it from exploding.

Nathan laid a hand on her mother's shoulder. "I'll get the nurse." He stepped from the room quietly.

Camille asked her mother, "Who is that?"

Her mother gripped Camille's hand tighter, and her words were full of sadness. "That's Nathan, your stepfather."

Camille wasn't sure she had a stepfather. The man looked familiar, but she didn't know him like she would a stepdad.

The urgency to ask again hit her. "Where is the man?"

The image of the man came to her again. This time, the vision was clearer. He had dark hair and broad shoulders that blocked most of the light shining behind him, but he was still frantic. She felt the urgent need to tell him she didn't want to leave him. It would calm his panic.

"I don't know, sweetie." Her mom turned toward the door. "Where is that nurse?"

"Where is the man?" Camille asked again, her volume rising.

"The doctor said the confusion would be normal." Her mother looked as if she were trying to convince herself more than Camille.

"He's afraid." She knew it in her bones, and her

heart was beating faster as she grew frantic. He was real. *Was it a memory?* Yes, an important one.

She was confused, and the man's fear in the vision suddenly became her own. Her voice shook as she asked, "Mom? What happened?"

Her mom was crying in earnest by the time the nurse and Nathan stepped into the room.

"Don't worry, Mrs. Vanderbilt," the nurse addressed her mother. "Doctor Gould is on his way."

The nurse began asking Camille questions, and the only answer she knew for sure was yes, she was in pain.

Within minutes, the pain receded, and Camille fell into the darkness.

C amille woke slowly to the sounds of multiple voices.

The worried look on her mother's face grew as a man holding a tablet pecked away at the screen.

"We're not sure of anything yet, Mrs. Vanderbilt. We've had a few glimpses of consciousness that have shown us the possibility of memory loss, but each brain injury is different. Observing her will be the best indicator of the severity of her memory loss."

Bonnie nervously tugged at the collar of her shirt. "Why did she remember me and not Nathan?"

"Like I said, it's impossible to know," the young man wearing a white coat said. "Memory loss usually affects the short-term memory more than long-term. You should expect her to forget things such as where she parked her car, to attend appointments, to return phone calls, and where she left her purse."

The other man spoke up. "But what about people?"

Her mother placed a comforting hand on the man's shoulder. "Right, Nathan has been her step-father for twelve years. How could she forget him?"

"Memory loss is unpredictable. She may remember phone numbers better than people. She may remember places or work clients more than her own family. It's impossible to say until she sustains consciousness and the neurologist can evaluate her condition."

Her mother glanced her way and gasped. "She's awake. Camille, how are you feeling?"

Camille studied the people in the room, unsure of what to say. "I don't feel great." She felt tired, but she'd just woken up.

The young man tapped on the screen of his tablet. "I'll let Dr. Gould know she's awake."

"Thank you," her mother offered over her shoulder. Her attention never strayed from Camille's face.

"I'm okay, Mom. I just don't feel the best."

Camille closed her eyes against the bright lights. "You don't have to worry."

"Of course, I do. I love you so much." Camille's mother hugged her gently.

"I love you too."

She didn't want to think about what might come next. She had her mother beside her, and she was happy.

Camille felt a wave of peace wash over her as she heard her mother's whispered prayers. Everything would be all right. She had to hold on to that hope.

CHAPTER 5
NOAH
SIX MONTHS LATER

Noah's phone dinged as he stepped through the door of Sticky Sweets Bakery. He scrambled to pull the phone from his pocket. He knew it was Jenny. Her morning updates about Camille's recovery were like clockwork, and he lived for those bits of information. If he couldn't be there with Camille himself, hearing from Jenny that Camille was doing well was the next best thing.

Jenny: Our girl is good. Starting back to work this morning.

Someone shoved his shoulder, and he turned to see Lucas following him. Most of their crew members stopped by Sticky Sweets for coffee before the grind of the shift. The owner, Tracy, was a good friend of his mom, and she always threw in a cream cheese Danish for him if she was working the register. Those treats were certainly worth the extra hours in the gym.

Lucas pointed toward the growing line. "Migrate, man. We got somewhere to be." Their shift didn't start for another hour, but they all liked to arrive early. He leaned in closer and whispered, "Plus, look who's working today." Lucas waved at Victoria, a young barista he often flirted with. He made eyes at lots of women but rarely took them on dates. He was the fun, playful type, but settling down wasn't on Lucas's radar.

Noah wasn't usually one to lag, but he was exhausted today. He couldn't remember the last time he'd slept through the night, but Camille's piercing green eyes filled his dreams when he'd finally crashed the night before.

"Sorry." Noah stepped up behind the last person in line and looked back at the text from Jenny.

Maybe the lack of sleep was really getting to him. He needed some coffee in his system soon because he was sure Jenny's update had to be wrong.

Noah: Did she leave? Why didn't you tell me?

If she was working again, did that mean she was back in Portland? Just because he hadn't talked to Camille in years didn't mean he hadn't kept his ears open to anything she might be doing.

He locked his phone and returned his gaze to the busy bakery waiting area. He needed something to distract him from the message he'd just read. He could feel his heartbeat racing against the invisible anxiety.

"You okay, man?" Lucas tilted his head slightly and his brow furrowed. "You don't look so good."

"Yeah, just a text from Jenny."

"Camille okay?" Lucas asked. He knew a little about the situation with Camille and her recovery.

"I don't know. I guess." Noah didn't like to talk about it, so Lucas was smart enough to give him his space most of the time.

Noah checked his phone again. Why wasn't Jenny responding?

They made it to the counter and placed their orders before stepping to the side to wait for their coffee. Noah was still waiting for a text from Jenny when a woman squeezed into the small space beside him and grabbed the chai latte the barista extended to her.

"Thanks. I'll see you tomorrow," the customer said in a cheery sweet tone.

Noah turned at the sound of the familiar voice that sent his heart racing for the finish line.

Camille gasped when she saw him. Mouth hanging slightly open, she seemed timid and vulnerable in a way he never thought he'd see.

She tilted her head and said, "It's you!"

He wanted to say something, but her voice paralyzed him. He'd heard it in his dreams for years, and now she was here—standing in front of him as if she hadn't just rocked his world.

She was even more beautiful than he remembered. Her long dark hair was pulled back into a ponytail that gathered on the left side of her neck and fell in waves down her shoulder. Those green eyes that kept him up at night were vibrant and wide beneath thin brows as they stared back at him.

She looked relieved and surprised as she smiled and said, "I've been looking for you."

He still wasn't sure what to say. Jenny had told him Camille had lost a lot of her memory, but things were coming back in bits and pieces. She still had good days and bad days.

Terrified of the answer, he'd been too scared to ask Jenny if Camille remembered him. He'd prayed for this moment, but he'd dreaded it at the same time.

Camille placed a warm hand on his arm, and his senses flared into overdrive.

Some things never changed.

"I needed to tell you that I—" Camille's expression morphed into one of confusion. "I didn't want to leave you." Her voice trailed off at the end as if she wasn't sure she was saying the right thing.

Those were the words he'd wanted to hear for years. Now, his mouth turned up in a slow smile. "Really?"

Camille nodded and averted her gaze. Was she

embarrassed? His Camille was never afraid to put it all out there—proud to be herself.

She glanced at his chest and read the words on his navy shirt. "Blackwater Fire Department. You must've been there after my wreck."

Noah's smile faltered. She *didn't* remember him. Not really.

Camille went on, still holding his arm. "When I woke up, the only thing I remembered was your face."

Good grief, this was so much harder than he thought it would be. Did she remember everything about him or just that moment from the ambulance?

Camille pulled her hand away from his arm and self-consciously brushed a stray hair from her face. "And I thought I remembered you saying..."

He couldn't do this much longer. His heart was breaking. "What?"

"I thought you said, 'Don't leave me,' but that doesn't sound right." She shook her head and frowned.

"I did." He hated that confused look on her face. Jenny was going to get an earful for not telling him Camille's memory was still so unstable. He reached for her arm, and she didn't pull away when he touched her. "I did say that. You really scared me."

Camille perked up. "I thought so!" Her tone was lighter, and she sounded more like the fiery Camille he knew.

She continued, "Anyway, I couldn't say anything then, but I was trying to tell you that I didn't want to leave. I don't think I was scared, but... you were, and I thought it was important that I tell you that." She looked confused again and placed a hand on her forehead. "I'm sorry. This must sound crazy. I had a head injury, and my memory has been—"

"You don't have to explain, Camille." He wanted to hold her. He wanted to reassure her that he understood everything about her, and everything would be all right. Traumatic brain injuries were not to be taken lightly, and each case was unique.

But that look of confusion was back in her eyes. "You know me?" She said the words slowly as if tasting them on her tongue.

It wasn't really a question. She was telling herself. "I don't remember your name. I lost a lot of my memories." Her expression was apologetic.

"I'm Noah. We were..." There wasn't a real word to describe what they were. "Friends."

"Friends?" she questioned, tilting her head down and raising her perfectly arched eyebrows in disbelief.

"Best friends," Noah amended.

She was confused, and Noah wanted to brush the crease from between her brows.

"It's hard to tell what's a dream and what's a memory, you know?" She shook her head. "Of course, you don't know. I sound like a lunatic." She plastered on a fake smile and shrugged.

"No, no! You don't. It makes perfect sense." Everything about Camille had always made sense to him. "I was there after your wreck. I just didn't know you didn't remember more about me." It was the truth. He hadn't known for sure. What worried him most were the memories she'd lost about *them*.

Lucas stepped up beside him. "Hey, I got yours too. Ready to go?" He noticed Camille, and his eyes bulged. "Oh, I'll just... wait over here... within hearing distance."

Lucas was anything but subtle.

Noah turned his attention back to Camille. She was beautiful and scared, and his heart was still racing from her proximity.

His past with her felt fragile. Was it even real if she didn't share those memories too? It was as if their lives together were suddenly erased.

He wasn't sure if he should feel distraught or relieved. There were so many things he wished she remembered about their past, but there were some things he wished they could both forget.

This was a second chance. He could use it to start over with her and get things right.

But the forces that stood between them were still alive and well.

What if she didn't have the same feelings for him that she used to? What if she'd already moved on before her injury? He couldn't force her to love him again just because he couldn't stop loving her. His feelings for her had only grown, but how would he ever know where she'd stood before her memory was scrambled?

He couldn't act like it didn't tear him apart to be away from her.

"What *kind* of friends were we?" Camille asked.

He knew she was asking if they were *more* than friends, but he wasn't sure how to answer. He knew what he *wanted* to say, but that might not be right anymore.

He was suddenly aware that they were standing together in a crowded bakery at the busiest time of the day, and as much as he wanted to tell the world that he was lucky to stand next to Camille Vanderbilt, her stepdad, Nathan, wouldn't be happy.

Possibly unhappy enough to carry out his threat.

"It's kind of a long story." Noah glanced around the bakery to see who was watching them. Lucas was propped against a nearby wall and might as well have popcorn. He was invested in the private conversation Noah was trying to have with Camille.

Jenny said Camille was starting a job, but she was here, so maybe that was grounds for hope. "Are you going to be around later in the week?" Noah asked.

Lucas made a jerking motion with his head indicating they needed to be heading out.

"I'm back in town indefinitely. My parents have been helping me out during recovery, but I just rented a house outside of town. That's where I'll be until I find something permanent." She hooked her thumb over her shoulder. "I start work at Black-water Restoration today. You know, the thrift store."

He had a moment of internal celebration before he replied, "Good. I'll be volunteering there on Thursday."

"Really?" She perked up.

It did something crazy to his heart to know she was excited to see him again. "Yeah. I usually make time to go by once a week and help move around the heavier things. I'll see you then."

Lucas was being obvious about getting to work now. His gestures and facial expressions were getting out of hand. People would start gawking soon.

Noah smiled at Camille. Knowing he'd see her again after his shift put pep in his step. "Maybe we can talk more then."

"Great!"

Her smile was back, and he might have imagined the sweep of her gaze down his frame and then back up.

"I need to get to work. See you soon." He nodded at her as if tipping a cowboy hat. The movement was almost second nature.

As if startled out of a daze, she jerked. "Oh! I

need to get to work too. Really unprofessional for the new manager to be late on her first day." She gave him a tempting wink as she stepped around him.

Rooted in place, he watched her walk all the way out of the bakery. Had he really just talked to Camille?

Lucas rushed over. "Dude! Move your feet. I'm not getting a tongue lashing from Cap because you were drunk on puppy love."

Noah followed Lucas out of the bakery. He checked his phone for the time and noticed a text from Jenny.

Jenny: She's here. Don't worry.

The only thing he was worried about was being away from Camille again. He hadn't wanted to let her go—now or six years ago.

One thing was certain, he couldn't let her get away again. He had to find a way to be with her without the threat from her stepdad hanging over his head.

CHAPTER 6
CAMILLE

"I *know* he's important, Jen." Camille balanced the phone between her ear and shoulder as she typed in the data from the last donation.

Jenny sighed on the other end of the call. "You're right. He *is* important. I just don't know how to tell you about him. He's... different."

Camille agreed. She hadn't been able to stop thinking of Noah since he'd said his name at Sticky Sweets at the beginning of the week. His dark, expressive eyes were hard to forget. The more she thought about him, the more she remembered that stubbled jaw and broad nose.

She'd been all but obsessing over the man in her dreams for months, and it'd been a shock to run into the handsome firefighter in town. She'd been describing the man in her dreams to Jenny since the accident, and her cousin hadn't let on that it might be someone that Camille used to know.

"I'll say," Camille agreed. "But it doesn't matter what kind of different he is. I need to remember how I knew him."

Camille's dreams had morphed from the shadowed vision she'd first remembered and now included Noah in various parts of everyday life. She thought she recalled horseback riding with him, fishing, standing beside him at her locker at a school, and even laughing with him. The dreams were always full of happiness, but they might have been just that—dreams, not recollections. She wasn't sure how to determine the difference.

"I get it. I wish I could help, but I think this is something you need to remember on your own. I can't tell you what you and Noah were like back then. I was there, but just trust me, it was... special. I can't intrude on those memories with my own observations."

Camille saved the spreadsheet she was working on and stood up, reaching for her cup of coffee. She needed to unlock the front door before opening hours. "I understand, but it's so frustrating having to wait on my own brain to fill in the blanks."

Even small tasks were frustrating these days. The neurologist assured her that memory loss recoveries were unique to each patient, but she was getting tired of forgetting her work schedule and things like returning her mother's phone calls.

"I bet. You've always liked to be in control, and I can imagine this is the worst for you. If it makes you feel any better, I can vouch for Noah. He's a really great guy. The three of us spent a lot of time together when we were younger. He always put you first." Jenny's voice softened and trailed off on the last word. "Noah is the most selfless person I know. He'd do anything for someone who needed help."

The ding of the bell above the front door chimed, and Camille stepped from her office behind the register into the main room, sure she'd locked the door behind her when coming in this morning.

She released the heavy breath she'd been holding when she saw Noah walk in. Her stomach tumbled, and a smile took up residence on her face.

"I've got to go," Camille whispered to Jenny. "I'll call you later."

Camille barely heard Jenny's "Bye" as she disconnected the call.

Camille couldn't take her eyes off the gorgeous man walking toward her. His smile reflected her own, and his dark eyes held a key to the past. She knew those eyes like she knew her own name. The brown reminded her of the color of the dirt on the worn trails where she used to ride horses… with him.

Sometimes it was hard to decide if the visions

floating in her head were recollections of dreams or flashes of forgotten realities. There were some things she knew for sure. She'd definitely been horseback riding with this man before.

But in her memories, he was leaner, and his features weren't so stern. The boy in her dreams looked like a carefree version of the man standing in front of her now, though his smile was still soft and kind.

"Morning." His voice was deep, and the timbre rolled over her, settling in her chest.

"Good morning, stranger."

Was he always punctual or was he eager to see her? "We got a big intake yesterday evening with a bedroom set." She thrust a thumb over her shoulder. "Care to help me move them?" The thrift store received donations daily, and she knew Noah's strength was invaluable in moving the larger pieces.

Noah nodded, and his smile didn't waver. "Put me to work, boss."

"I thought you could spill your darkest secrets to me while we work. For some reason, no one wants to enlighten me about anything to do with *us*."

The word "us" had her stomach flipping as if it didn't know which way was up.

He fell into step beside her as they made their way to the delivery room. His steps were loud and heavy in the quiet store. He was real this time, not a dream, standing tall beside her in a heather-gray thermal shirt that hugged his muscular shoulders all too well. Her nose was level with the top of his broad shoulders when she turned toward him.

"You mean Jenny didn't tell you?" he asked.

She could hear the caution in his words. "Nope. Some kin she is," Camille said in mock irritation. "She said I need to remember you on my own."

"I can't argue with that, but I'd be happy to help you remember."

Camille looked at him to gauge his sincerity and found him staring back at her. He gave her a playful wink, and she wondered what she'd stumbled into at Sticky Sweets Bakery.

The lighthearted attitude seemed to fall from his face as he continued, "And I imagine she didn't want to upset your stepdad."

Nathan again. She knew her stepdad had a big hand in most things regarding her, but she was beginning to see the huge thumb he'd pressed on her life. She wasn't sure about her feelings for Nathan yet, but she wondered how much he'd influenced the decisions she'd made in the past. Apparently, he'd even coerced her into a career in corporate law, something she couldn't imagine enjoying or having a true passion to pursue.

She supposed that didn't matter now. She'd resigned from her position at Parker and Lions when she'd recovered enough from her injury to know that she wasn't interested in going back. The awful anxiety she felt every time she thought of the place only filled her with dread.

Not that she remembered how to do her job anyway. She supposed if she immersed herself in corporate law again, she could remember, but she had no desire to do that. When she'd realized she had enough money to get by until she could find a new career path, she'd quit Parker and Lions. She'd picked up some study materials when her doctor had suggested reviewing old texts that might spark recollections.

Camille wanted to stay in Blackwater anyway. She loved it here and wanted to be closer to her mom and Jenny. She wasn't sure why she'd left in the first place, but she had a hunch it had something to do with her stepdad.

Camille watched Noah as they made their way through the store. She wondered what kind of relationship they'd really had before, if any. Surely, if he'd cared for her, they'd still be together. Or had they ever been together at all? Had they truly only been friends like he said? It didn't seem right. The ghost of the feelings she felt for him were more than just friendly feelings.

Maybe he just hadn't been as interested in her as she was in him. She was quirky on a good day, and he seemed reserved. Maybe he preferred blondes.

They entered the intake room and Camille pointed toward the furniture. "There. It needs to go to the far west wall." She grabbed one side of the headboard while he took the other. It was crazy heavy, but he made it look easy. Her pride had her determined to make it all the way to the west wall without asking for a break, and she was gasping for air by the time they dropped the heavy piece in its new place.

Back in the intake room, Noah was quick to lift the nightstand on his own and shoo her out of his way with his chin as he relocated the piece on his own.

Camille couldn't do anything except watch him hulk out on the insignificant furniture. He threw it around like it weighed as much as cotton candy. Now she had man candy on the brain. She could really use a Snickers right about now.

"What's next, boss?"

Noah's voice had her jumping back into the here and now. "Um, I think that's all the heavy stuff for now. Can you help me stock the display by the front entrance?"

Noah nodded and followed her to the cart that housed the new items to go out.

"So," Camille began, "tell me something?"

"About you?" Noah asked.

"Sure. Let's start there."

"You sure you're ready for this?" His playful questioning was welcome.

Everyone else walked on eggshells around her.

She liked it when he pushed her. "If you can give it, I can take it."

Noah seemed to ponder his answer as he arranged the glassware on the table. "Well, you were always up for an adventure. Anything outdoors." He kept his head down, but his eyes turned up to her. "You were sassy... and witty." He said the words almost as if he were testing the waters between them. "You were incredibly smart but impulsive."

"Me? No," Camille joked. He seemed to know specific details about her, and the thought had her hopes running wild.

"It's true. You got us in trouble a few times."

"I don't want to hear your Debbie Downer stories," Camille countered. "Tell me about you." She really wanted to hear more about the *us* he'd mentioned.

"What I was like with you?" he asked.

Yes, she wanted to know what he was like with her. Had he been different with her?

"Yeah. Start there."

"I was happy... and scared." Again, his words were laced with caution.

"What were you afraid of?" She might be sealing her fate, but she had to know.

Noah's gaze lifted to her, but his words were quiet. "I was afraid to hope it would last. That we'd just stay the way we were."

Camille swallowed the lump in her throat and asked, "Were we *together*?"

He smiled, and her fears seemed to flee. "It depends on who you ask and when."

She felt a sting of hurt at his dismissal, and a flash of anger lit her heart. "That's super vague, storyteller. This isn't mystery theater. I want a biography."

Seeming to understand her hurt, he leaned his strong arms on the table and leveled her with a serious stare. "I could write your biography. Don't misunderstand me."

Camille focused her attention on the task in front of her.

After a few seconds of silence, Noah stopped and said, "Listen, it wasn't because I didn't want us to be *more*. We just had different lives."

Camille gritted her teeth and nodded. "How so?"

"Women like you don't love men like me, Camille."

The hurt in his voice made her stop. When she looked up at him, the crease between his brows disappeared and he plastered on a fake smile. She wanted to tell him he didn't know enough about her to make that call, but she wasn't sure of much these days, and her uncertainties kept her silent.

She wondered if Nathan had anything to do with the rift between Noah and herself. The words almost ripped themselves from her throat, but she choked them back, afraid of the answer.

"I feel like we were more," Camille confessed. "It's just a hunch, but I feel like there's much more to remember about you."

Noah's fake smile morphed into something gentle and real. "There's a lot more." His dark eyes shifted from her self-consciously before he cleared his throat and asked, "Why are you working here? Aren't you an attorney?"

"How'd you know that?" Camille asked.

He knew way more about her than she realized.

"It's what you planned to major in when you went off to college."

Maybe they'd drifted apart because she'd left for college. It happened to lots of people. Had she been the one to tear a hole in whatever they'd had back then? How did someone she knew six years ago remember her college major?

"I am an attorney. I worked at a corporate firm in Portland. After the wreck, it was a long time before I could go back to work. By the time I was able to, I remembered enough about my job to know that I didn't want to work there anymore. I had options, and I wasn't going back to Parker and Lions."

She couldn't bring herself to admit to him that she hadn't completely remembered how to do her job. "I didn't remember much about it. Mostly feelings, but they weren't pleasant."

"Uh-oh," Noah added, as if the audience director had held up a sign for his cue.

"I want my work to be important to me. *This* feels important."

Noah nodded. "It's important to me too. That's why I volunteer. We see a lot of families who suddenly find themselves with nothing."

"So, you're a firefighter and you volunteer on your off days? What a hero." Camille threw her hand over her forehead and feigned swooning.

Noah chuckled. "Sort of. I only volunteer here one day a week, and I work at the ranch on the other days. I work two days on and four days off with the fire department."

Camille concentrated as the mention of a ranch sparked her memory. "Blackwater Ranch?"

Noah perked up. "Yeah. You remember?"

"I think I do!" Camille's excitement mirrored Noah's.

"It's about twenty miles outside of town. It's been in my family for five generations." The pride in his voice when he talked about his family filled her with happiness.

Then the emotion triggered a memory. She could remember lying on a boulder beside Noah, looking out at a vast sky of stars. She was sure that place had to be somewhere on Blackwater Ranch.

Camille remembered turning to Noah. The look

in his eyes said he loved her as much or more than she loved him.

Her whispered words to him in the darkness had been born of fear. "Don't fall in love with me."

Noah's expression didn't change, and he didn't say anything. They'd both known he already had, just as they'd both known she loved him. She'd known because her heart had felt it—his love.

Her next words had come with a warning, as a tear rolled down the side of her face, unseen by him in the shadows wrapped around them. "Because I'll break your heart long before you can break mine."

Noah didn't falter, so sure of himself in the darkness. "I'm the only person you don't have to protect yourself from."

Even in her innocence, Camille had nodded. "I know."

Now, she looked over the table at Noah—the man that the boy in her memory had grown into. She still felt that sense of surety when she was with him, but she didn't really know him anymore. How could she be sure she should trust it?

Noah's smile faded, possibly because her own had turned into a frown. The memory had only confused her. "I need to get back to the office. I have some phone calls to make."

Camille left the few items that remained on the cart with Noah and hurried to her office. She remembered why she hadn't wanted him to love her. She'd been terrified of losing him. Her heart ached with the memory of what she'd felt years ago on that boulder with Noah.

She knew in her heart that she hadn't been the one to sever their ties. She waited until the office door was closed before wiping the stray tear from where it rested atop her cheek. There was still something missing in their past, and she needed to find out what it was before she let Noah potentially hurt her again.

CHAPTER 7
CAMILLE

C amille slid across the hardwood floor of the kitchen in her fuzzy socks. The sticky note on her bathroom mirror this morning said today was her last scheduled follow-up appointment for her head injury, and it was a *glorious* day. She woke up with a spring in her step and a song in her heart. Coffee was brewing, birds were chirping in the warm sun, and Camille would be free of all restrictions soon.

She'd been released to return to work a month ago, and honestly, she felt like that should've been the end of it. She'd done everything her doctors had recommended to help recover her memory. Still, better to take the doctor's orders and show up for one last appointment.

The sticky notes were still plastered all over her house, and she kept the Bluetooth tracker on her keys and purse, but things were getting better. She wasn't ready to say she didn't need those crutches anymore, but maybe the puzzles and exercising were helping.

Camille's phone rang, and she bounded to it, kicking her feet up behind her with each step. It was Jenny. She checked on Camille every morning around this time.

"Hello, Sunshine!" Camille answered.

"Someone is in a fabulous mood."

"You bet your bottom dollar I am! Today is my last appointment. No more doctors." Hopefully, that meant less of her parents hanging over her as well.

"I know. I keep up. You're doing fine, and I've been praying you get an excellent report this morning."

Camille smiled. "Same, girl. Once the neurologist says I'm okay, I think everyone else will believe it. Apparently, it means nothing when I say it."

"I believe you. I know you're better. Do I need to come with you?" Jenny asked.

"No need. I'll be fine on my own. Guess what. I got a chance to talk to Noah." Camille had been itching to tell Jenny about the memories. There were only a few, but they were special to her.

"Really? Tell me more."

Jenny had been understanding about Camille's new obsession with Noah Harding. But she still needed to find out why her friend had advised her not to talk to her parents about him. She wanted to have that conversation with Jenny in person. Camille suspected it had something to do with Nathan's controlling hand.

"We really were close back then, but you already know that. I did have a memory about us while we were talking."

"Was it a good one?" Jenny asked.

"Well, it was a confusing one." Camille bent to slip her tennis shoes on. "I told him not to fall in love with me." The emotions that the memory conjured were fresh as she recalled the vision. "I can't imagine why I wouldn't want him to love me. Especially since I think he did."

"Oh, Millie. I wish I could help you, but there were so many things between the two of you that only you know. Well, only you *knew*."

A knock sounded at Camille's door, and she frowned. "Hey, I need to let you go. Someone's at the door, and I'm not expecting anyone."

"Oh, no you don't! I'm staying on the phone until you know it's not a creeper."

Camille laughed but stayed on the call. She peered through the peephole and saw her mom on the other side of the door.

Her spirits died as she breathed, "I gotta go, Jen. It's Mom."

"Oh," was all Jenny said.

"Yeah. I'll call you after the appointment to let you know how it went," Camille promised.

She opened the door and tried not to think the worst. "Hey, is everything okay?"

Her mom smiled and lifted her shoulders a few times in excitement. "Of course. Your last appointment is this morning! I'll drive."

Camille took a deep breath as she prepared for the conversation that really needed to happen. "Mom, I can go alone."

Bonnie waved a manicured hand at her daughter. "No way. Nathan thinks I should go with you, and you know he always has your best interest at heart." She stepped close to Camille and rubbed her shoulder. "He thought you'd need your mother with you."

Camille always felt guilty asking her parents for independence. They really did mean well, but she was twenty-four. She'd been living on her own for years before the accident. She wasn't completely sure about how she'd felt about her independence before the wreck, but now, it was becoming more and more precious as it faded into a memory.

"That's sweet, but I'm okay to go by myself."

Her mother's brows knitted together. "I just want to make sure you're okay. Nathan does too. We know you need us more during this time."

Camille focused on controlling her breathing.

When would everyone stop treating her like a child? Especially her parents. Sometimes, it felt as if they weren't paying attention to the progress she was actually making. The doctor's reports carried more weight.

If she thought about it, most of her mom's overbearing acts led back to Nathan, and Camille still wasn't sure how she felt about her stepdad. Had she always harbored confused feelings about him?

Judging from the decisions she'd made in the past, it seemed like Nathan's influence had been in every piece of her life. She'd gone to college on the west coast, gotten a degree in law like him, and worked for a corporate firm tearing down small businesses.

Not one of those things sounded like the best path for her. They didn't support her dreams and the causes she felt so strongly about. If she was an attorney, why wasn't she practicing family law?

History proved Camille might have folded to Nathan's every whim in the past. Why had she done that? Had she done those things willingly? How had he convinced her to do those things unless they were important to her?

Now, that seemed foolish. Maybe growing up with him and knowing he had her best interest in mind had forged a different mindset for her before the accident.

These days, she wasn't so sure how she felt about him, but that wasn't a reason to send her mother away this morning after she'd driven all the way here to help Camille. She needed to remind herself that not everyone was blessed with parents who cared as much as hers.

Bonnie stroked Camille's shoulder, and a look of concern coated her mother's face. "Are you okay? Are the headaches back?"

"No, I'm fine." Camille must have been frowning again. "Let's go. If we leave now, we can grab breakfast on the way."

Her mother perked up, unaware that Camille's former elation was shattered.

She locked the door behind her and prayed that the report from the doctor would be a good one. It would devastate Camille if her mother were present to hear the medical professional's opinion that she wasn't progressing in her healing as expected.

CHAPTER 8
NOAH

Noah trudged into the main house and toed off his boots just as his brother, Aaron, pulled up and parked his pickup. All of the Harding brothers knew to leave the space closest to the door for Aaron so he could carry his son, Levi, inside. Days started early on the ranch, and Levi was a sound sleeper for a three-year-old. No one saw a reason to wake the kid at five in the morning.

Dixie panted, wagging her tail and bouncing from side to side.

"Hey, girl." Noah squatted to scratch the dog's head. The border collie was a trained wrangler, and she sure helped out when it came to moving the herds.

Stepping from the light-blue dusk into the meeting room of his parents' house, Noah hung his walnut-colored cowboy hat on the rack by the door.

It was more of a dining hall, but they always discussed chores and family topics during meals when they were all together. The first floor of what they all called the main house was made up of one cavernous meeting room on one side with wooden walls and high ceilings, while the other side was a large kitchen, a bathroom, a laundry room, and a cozy sitting room at the back. The upstairs consisted of four bedrooms and four bathrooms.

Noah spotted his mom stacking up plates at the end of the serving counter. Anita Harding had her graying black hair pulled into a bun atop her head and wore an apron with horses on it. Their dad had given it to her two Christmases ago, and she'd worn it every day since.

Meals were easier for everyone if they ate all at once as a family. Noah and his brothers used to take turns helping their mom with meal prep, but now their dad, Silas, helped out in the kitchen. Since his heart attack last year, he'd stepped back from a lot of the ranching duties, and his parents had decided they wanted to renovate the extra upstairs rooms in the main house to rent out in the winter months.

"Good morning," his mother shouted as Noah strode across the big room. His parents lived in the main house, but it was large enough to have lots of uses. A hundred years ago, the meeting room had still functioned as a cafeteria. The kitchen had been remodeled thirty years ago, and the ice house had been turned into a storage and freezer shed.

"Morning, Mom." Noah bent to wrap his mom in a one-arm hug. "Thanks for breakfast."

"Thank the good Lord for providing. It's bacon and eggs."

His dad walked in carrying a tray of scrambled eggs. The tray looked heavy, but Noah would stub his toe on a bedpost before he did something like offer to carry something for Silas Harding. Noah came from a long line of hardworking men. Pride was silent but understood.

"The eggs look good. They come from the Lawrence farm?" Noah asked.

"Sure did. I don't know what kind of gold they feed those chickens, but they lay the best eggs." Silas set the tray on the serving counter and scratched his stubbled chin.

Aaron walked in with Levi's sleeping form cradled to his chest. The kid could sleep through a stampede, so Noah and his parents didn't bother quieting their voices.

"You need any help with the house tomorrow?" It was Noah's last day off before his shift at the fire station, so if anything needed his attention at the ranch for the next few days, he needed to address it.

His dad tilted his head in thought. "I think Hunter is installing the new ceiling fans today. We picked up the paint yesterday, so the walls could use their first coat." Hunter was Noah's cousin who lived and worked on the ranch just like the five brothers.

Aaron laid Levi in his cot by the window and joined them at the bar. "I still can't believe we're selling out. We don't have to be a dude ranch just because everyone else around here is." Aaron grabbed a plate from the stack.

Their mother swatted Aaron's hand. "Put that down. No one eats until the whole family is here."

Aaron eyed the door. "They better come on. I need to split the north herd before the dew dries. We're baling today when the sun gets high."

The front door opened, and the remaining brothers entered. Lucas led the pack, smiling. "Let's eat, boys."

Their father stepped back, always last to make his way through the meal lines, but the men gave way for their mom to go first. Noah fell in line behind his mom at the serving bar.

She inched her way closer to him and said, "So, I saw Camille Vanderbilt when we were picking up the paint."

Noah shifted his gaze from the plate full of eggs to his mother. "Oh, yeah? What'd she have to say?" He tried to keep his voice casual, as if talking about Camille were the most normal thing to do with his mother.

"She didn't see me, but I suspect she might not

have known me if she had. Has she gotten her memory back?"

Noah had told his mom about the call and Camille's accident six months ago. His mom also knew he got regular updates from Jenny, but he hadn't yet told his family he'd been working with his old best friend.

"Not exactly. She remembers some things, but not everything." He couldn't look at his mom as they spoke now. This wasn't something he wanted to talk about.

"I suspect she'll remember you one day. Don't give up hope."

How did his mom know he even wanted to be remembered? For all she knew, he'd severed all connection with his friend six years ago when she'd gone off to college. Granted, that was his fault for being too ashamed to tell her *why* he'd cut Camille out of his life.

"She might." Noah shrugged and hoped to leave the conversation there.

Lucas piped up farther down the line. "Yeah, she sure looked like she wanted to know more about you when we ran into her at Sticky Sweets the other day."

Asher turned to Noah. "Is that right? So, our little Millie is making a comeback?"

Noah's brothers were familiar with his old

friend. They probably knew how he still felt about her, though no one talked about it directly.

Noah shook his head. "You know she hates it when you taunt her with that name." She liked it when Noah or Jenny called her Millie, but Camille always said it sounded like a joke coming from anyone else.

Granted, Noah had always felt special that she allowed him to give her a welcome nickname. He never wanted her to feel picked on because of her name or who she was.

"What do you know about what she hates these days?" Asher quipped. "*She* doesn't even know."

Micah, their eldest brother, reached around Lucas to swat Asher in the back of the head. "Knock it off." Micah was broad and thick like their mom's folks, while Asher was tall and lean like their dad's side of the family.

Asher was right. What would she think about the nickname now? Noah's mother reached over and laid a hand on his shoulder.

"Don't lose hope, son. We all love Camille, whether she remembers us or not. If it's the Lord's will for things to work out between the two of you, nothing will stop it."

Noah kept quiet through the rest of the line. The family rule was to wait for everyone to be seated before their father prayed.

With every head bowed, Silas began. "Our most gracious Father, we humble ourselves before You, asking for Your guidance and blessing as we go about our day. We pray for healing for Camille as she navigates these uncertain times. Please bless this food to our bodies and our bodies to Your service. In Jesus' name, I pray and ask these things. Amen."

Noah lifted his head and glanced at his dad. Silas Harding heard everything but said little. His words were reserved but powerful. The whole Harding family *did* care about Camille. She'd been as much a part of this ranch as the fences at one time, and Noah's heart ached to see her home again.

CHAPTER 9
NOAH

The next week, Noah balanced two to-go cups of coffee on his arm as he unlocked the door to Blackwater Restoration. It was early, but he'd bet his last paycheck that Camille was already in her office.

The bell chimed above the door as he entered, and Camille peeked her head out of the office doorway before he'd taken five steps.

"Morning," she greeted him. "You're here early."

Noah's heartbeat fluttered in his chest. He'd never get used to her beauty. It knocked him on his rear end every time he saw her. Her dark hair hung in waves over her shoulder, and her straight nose slanted down toward her thin lips.

"Morning, sunshine."

Camille met him by the register, and he extended one of the cups to her. She lit up with a smile that filled her whole face. The mounds of her cheeks lifted, and her eyes almost squinted with the expression.

"And that's how I know you're special."

He wasn't sure where this was going, but he was more than happy to follow. "How?"

"You make me smile before I've had coffee." Her eyes sparkled in the morning sun streaming through the open shop windows.

The last thing Noah wanted to be was the darkness that put out Camille's light. There was still something between them, but every word, every look, every moment between them was a balancing act. He was constantly afraid of sending her running the way she had last week.

He wasn't sure what he'd said or done, but after their morning talk, she hadn't ventured out of her office much. She seemed to have forgiven him for whatever wrong he'd done, and he was grateful.

She could walk away from him, but loving her wasn't something he could stop. It would happen whether he wanted it to or not. The sun was meant to shine, and Noah Harding was meant to love Camille Vanderbilt. There was no sense in fighting it. It was just going to be difficult to explain that to her when she certainly didn't love him—or even know him—yet.

Noah realized he'd gotten lost in a daydream and shook his head to regain his composure. He'd been staring, and he'd moved to stand a bit too close to her. He took one small step back.

"What's on the list for today?" he asked.

Camille shrugged. She was much more relaxed today. "The Cody location is sending a shipment today. Not much is happening until they deliver at noon."

Camille's phone rang in her back pocket, and she pulled it out to look at it and stuck it back in her pocket without answering.

Noah was standing close enough that he'd seen "Mom" at the top of the screen. Camille had always been close to her mother, and he couldn't imagine why she hadn't just taken the call.

"You can answer that." The store wasn't even open yet, but Kathy, the owner, had lenient policies regarding phones.

"Nah." Camille turned away from him and picked up a dust rag. "It's Mom. She's hovering. I've already talked to her twice today."

That sounded like Bonnie to worry. "She just cares."

"I know."

He grabbed a rag and followed Camille to the front of the store. The bright June sunshine was warm through the large windows. "How are things with your mom?" He hoped it wasn't too forward, but he'd known their family for half of his life.

"Fine. Mostly. I'm still recovering in lots of ways,

but Mom and Nathan aren't progressing with me. I feel like I'm back to good, but they still see me as a lesser version of what I was before the wreck. I'm okay with the slow recovery... most days. I still forget things like calling my mom back or where I parked my car, but those are things I can manage. The doctors assure me that the short-term memory problems shouldn't last forever."

Getting updates from Camille was very different from getting updates from Jenny. Jenny's updates had been hopeful and reassuring. Hearing Camille talk about her daily struggles was much more harrowing.

She continued, "Can't they understand? I'll never be finished with myself. I'm allowed to be complete but still getting stronger."

"I get it. You'll be catching up and growing at the same time."

"Exactly!" Camille's eyes bulged, and she waved the dust rag in the air. "I feel like I'm the same, but I don't know all of what I was like before. I just know that I don't want to take a single thing for granted now." Camille rubbed the rag over an empty shelf. "Life can be incredibly short, and God has given me so much already."

He moved closer to her, dusting the shelf beside her.

Her voice dipped even lower, and the whispers between them made the conversation feel like a secret. "I don't want God to think I'm bored here. I want more years in my life. I want a chance to do all the things I didn't before."

Her gaze tilted up to him, and he felt the urgency she spoke of. There were so many things he wanted to do with her, so much time to make up for now. He'd never hoped to get the second chance that stood before him now.

The burning desire to press his lips to hers was growing inside him. He was close enough that he could just lean in and erase the space between them. His gaze was locked on her smooth lips when she spoke.

"What do you do for fun?"

Noah sucked in a deep breath, his nostrils flaring. "I like my job. I'm probably one of the few who thinks going to work is fun."

Camille laughed, and he was back in a daydream. "What made you want to become a firefighter?"

She used to know the story, but he didn't mind telling her again. "When I was about six years old, there was a massive fire at the ranch. It leveled the main barn. I remember when the firefighters came to put out the flames. I knew then that I wanted to do that one day."

Camille stopped the waxing motion on the shelf in front of her. "I think I remember that. Or I remember you telling me about it."

The bell above the door chimed, and a thin, white-haired woman walked in.

"Hey there. Let me know if I can help you find anything," Camille said in greeting.

"Oh, I'm just looking for bedding."

Camille left her rag on the shelf and went to show the woman the bedding section.

Noah continued dusting, working his way along the shelves at the front of the store.

A few minutes later, Camille returned and picked up her work alongside him.

"What's it like when you remember things?" Noah asked.

Camille lifted her shoulders and let them fall. "It's kind of like there are a million tiny boxes inside my mind, but they're mostly locked." She looked up at him with a reserved grin. "When I get a memory, it's like a box decides to open, and I get a secret, an important secret that I don't know how I lived without before."

"I bet it's tough."

"It is. Especially when I'm not sure if the 'memory' was a real thing that happened or an old dream." She turned to him and slapped the dusty rag against his chest. "Enough somber talk. What else do you like to do?"

"I work the ranch on my days off."

"Ooh, sounds exciting."

Noah laughed at her reaction. "I guess so. Maybe

to some. Others might think it's backbreaking or rough. I like being outside, and I like working alone. Being on the ranch often lets me do both of those. It's not much, but it's my family's way of life."

Camille's carefree attitude was back now that they'd moved past the tough subject. She made a dramatic show of her reaction, and her whole face was animated. "Silly boy, you should think you're as awesome as I do."

Noah grabbed the rag in her hand and stilled. She'd said those words to him before, only a little different.

He could remember following Camille as she waded through the shallows of Bluestone Creek on the northern edge of the ranch. They'd been no more than seventeen, and Noah had been completely in love with Camille. He'd followed her everywhere.

Camille's long, dark hair streamed behind her in the summer breeze. He'd been grumbling about being a terrible fly fisher after she'd caught twice as many as him the day before.

She'd turned around to face him as she walked backward through the shallows. "Silly boy, one day you'll think you're as awesome as I do."

Her last word had been drawn out and loud as she'd fallen backward into the cold water. It had been early summer, and the water temperatures were barely tolerable.

Camille had laughed through her chattering

teeth as Noah scooped her up into his arms, and she hadn't protested as he'd carried her back to the truck and wrapped her in blankets.

Now, Noah pulled her in closer by the rag they both held. "Will you come to the ranch tonight?" It was more of a plea than a question.

Camille tried to hide her grin. "Okay." She stepped back and playfully tugged her rag from his grip, leaving him staring after her, barely breathing.

She turned to the next shelf and gasped. "Look!" She lifted a small, hand-painted vase.

Noah stepped closer to see that it was painted blues and greens with a lighter circle framing the silhouette of a young girl and a horse.

"I think I just found my soulmate," Camille stated. "The person who made this. Not the person who donated it," she pointed out. "That person is crazy."

Noah laughed and shook his head. "You're so simple."

She turned to him with a mischievous wink. "Said no one ever."

She was right. Camille Vanderbilt was anything but simple, but that was what he loved about her.

CHAPTER 10

CAMILLE

Camille peeked at the clock on the wall in her office and wondered if it was too early to mosey on over to the ranch. Noah said the whole family had supper together at six thirty in the evening, so this technically wasn't a date. Still, it didn't hurt anyone when she imagined that it *was* a date. It was a few minutes till five now, but she could take her time and familiarize herself with the area. He'd given her the address before he left the store around three in the afternoon.

She pulled out of the parking lot at Blackwater Restoration and followed the robotic directions from her 4Runner's built-in navigation system. She smiled every time she anticipated a turn before the voice told her where to go.

When she saw the rusted sign that said "Blackwater Ranch" at the end of a dirt road, she sat up straighter in her seat. The dash clock told her she was twenty minutes early, and she wasn't sure if Noah and his family were ready for her yet.

Camille parked her car near the entrance to a big house she recognized, and she breathed a sigh of relief when a gray-haired woman smiled and waved in greeting. That smile was too familiar. She was Noah's mother.

The more time Camille spent with Noah, the more her memory filled in the pieces of the puzzle around him. This place and the people here were more familiar to her than she'd expected.

Camille jumped from the car and turned in a circle to take in the wide-open ranch around her. The blue sky seemed vibrant next to the verdant hills.

"Hey there, Camille. Come on in. Noah told me you'd be joining us tonight." The woman extended a hand to Camille from the porch, and she padded over quickly to greet the slightly familiar friend.

"It's great to be here," Camille said in return. Truly, she felt a happiness bubbling up inside her. "I know you, but I don't recall your name."

The woman smiled, causing the crow's feet around her eyes to deepen. "That's all right. You didn't call me Anita much anyway. You always called me Mama Harding."

A familiarity rang in Camille's head at the name. "Sounds right to me. It's good to see you again,

Mama Harding." Without thinking, Camille leaned in and gave Noah's mom a full-on hug. She smelled flour in Mama Harding's hair, and Camille filled her lungs with the seemingly familiar scent. She wanted more of this. She wanted a life filled with tight hugs and blue skies.

Mama Harding pulled back and tilted her head. "Come on in. You can help me bring out the fixin's."

Camille followed the older woman to the kitchen at the back of a cavernous room filled with a long table and a bench seat on each side. A long counter ran along the far end of the room, and the kitchen lay just beyond that.

The delicious smells in the kitchen had Camille's mouth watering instantly. "Goodness, it smells amazing in here."

Mama Harding winked at her. "Just wait for dessert." She pointed toward a tray of cookies and leaned closer to Camille. "I'll let you have one now, but don't tell the men. The rule around here is no dessert until after the meal."

Camille didn't need to be told twice. She grabbed a cookie and shoved half of it into her mouth. Her eyes rolled and she sighed. "This is so good!" She waved the remaining half of the cookie in the air. "I remember this. How could I forget your oatmeal raisin cookies?"

Mama Harding nodded and picked up the massive tray of cornbread. "I knew I had to make them when Noah told me you were coming tonight."

Camille grabbed the glass bowl of mashed potatoes and followed Noah's mom out to the main room where they set them on the long bar. Once they were back in the kitchen, Camille asked, "Would you mind telling me a little bit about what Noah and I used to be like?" She waved her hands in the air to emphasize the generality of the question.

Mama Harding gave her a closed-mouth grin. "The two of you were inseparable. Since you were in middle school, I guess. You've been around here a long time."

Camille certainly felt like she'd been here before. How much she'd been here was what she didn't know. "And do you know anything about why we aren't close like that anymore?"

Mama Harding's mouth turned up on one side as the lines snaked across her forehead. "I wish I did, baby. Noah hasn't said hide nor hair about what happened after you left for college. All I know is it about tore my boy up on the inside."

Camille swallowed hard and grabbed a handful of tongs and serving spoons. "I was afraid of that."

"Whatever happened back then is in the past, and that means it don't matter much anymore. We're human, and we're bound to make mistakes, but we're also called to forgive each other. Now, I'm not sure which of you ended things, but I have a feeling it was Noah."

Camille's ears perked up at that. "What makes you think that?"

"You came by here once about three years ago looking for him." Mama Harding looked up at the ceiling as if she could see the scene play out over the wooden rafters. "You were fit to be tied, and you wanted to know why Noah wasn't talking to you."

"I still wish I knew why he was avoiding me and why he's suddenly being nice to me now." Camille scratched the back of her head and shrugged.

"You'll figure it out in time. Noah isn't one to talk your ears off, but he's like his daddy. He'll speak up when it's important."

The two women carried the meal supplies out to the main room. Camille studied the walls and the tiny nuances that brought the room to life. She was certain she knew this place—from the woven red-and-beige rug at the entrance to the rustic wagon wheel light fixtures. She felt welcomed here.

The door on the far side of the room opened, and Noah stepped in. Head down, his wide-brim cowboy hat covered his face, but she knew him by his stance. He carried his boots in one hand and set them beside the door before removing his hat and hanging it on the rack. She watched him run his hand through his hair then slap his hands on his dusty jeans.

He hadn't noticed her yet, but boy had she noticed him. He looked much more natural in a cowboy hat and worn boots. Why did seeing him in a cowboy hat make her want to tip it off his head and kiss him senseless? Camille rubbed her nervous hands over her cheeks before slipping them into the back pockets of her jeans.

When Noah looked up, his gaze landed on her as if she'd called his name. His smile grew with every step he took toward her, but she just stood there. Her mind was useless for anything except to watch him come to her.

"You're early."

Camille nodded. "Yeah, I was afraid I'd get lost." She shrugged and smiled. "But no worries. I didn't even need the GPS."

Noah narrowed his eyes at her. "Are you saying there are some things you can't forget?"

Stunned into speechlessness, Camille's mind wanted to agree with him. There *were* some things her mind refused to forget, like the way home.

"I guess so. Everything looked familiar on my way over."

Noah nodded. "I came in early to see if Mama needed a hand, but it looks like she already has you."

His mom stepped up beside them. "We've taken care of everything."

Noah lifted his hands then clenched them into fists. "I should wash up."

Camille reached for his hands. "Let me see."

He raised one eyebrow in question before slowly opening his hands in hers, palms up.

His hands were filthy. Calloused and cut, they were working hands. While Noah was ashamed of them, the sight drew her heart to him. Each scratch and cut reminded her of the labor and toil he continued day in and day out to make sure his family's ranch survived.

Not only that, but he still donated his time and what was left of his energy after his shift at the fire station. It just so happened that he gave what he could of himself to a cause that was close to her heart.

Camille had grown up with more than she could ever need, but that wasn't the case for so many, including Noah. Maybe that was the reason it was so important to her to give back what she could.

Noah stepped around Camille toward the washroom, but his gaze didn't leave her until he was craning his neck to hold a glimpse of her.

That man looked at her as if he knew the inner workings of her heart. Why did it feel as if he really did know more about her than he let on? All signs pointed to more than friends, but he'd been the one to introduce himself to her as an old friend, not an old boyfriend.

The rest of the Harding family filed into the room within the next few minutes, and they each introduced themselves to Camille. Some of the brothers seemed more comfortable with her than others, but maybe that was because they expected her to remember them.

Lucas and Asher were friendly and greeted her with smiles, while Aaron and Micah acknowledged her presence with a single nod. Hunter, Noah's cousin, was as tight-lipped as Aaron and Micah, but the imposing scar down the left side of his face might have had something to do with his cool greeting. He shifted to give her his profile before taking his place on the outskirts of the group.

The family talked and ate in peace around her, and no one made her feel unwelcome or uncomfortable. As she watched them go about their normal evening routine, she knew she'd been a part of the Harding suppers many times before. She fit in as if she belonged, and while Noah didn't speak much, his frequent glances her way told her he was keenly aware of her presence beside him.

CHAPTER 11
NOAH

If calm reserve hadn't been Noah's default, he wasn't sure he could've kept it together while eating supper beside Camille tonight. The casual scene was all too special to him to act as if nothing monumental was happening. Did she know how long he'd dreamed of spending evenings like this with her?

When they all finished eating, Aaron and Levi said their good-byes. The little guy had to get a bath and tucked into bed early. Noah watched Camille hug the toddler and whisper good night. Even though she put on a tough exterior, she'd always had a heart of gold.

Camille offered to help clean up after the meal, but Noah's mom shooed her away.

"Go on. You and Noah take the night off."

Asher looked around as if he didn't understand

what was going on. "Why do they get out of kitchen duty?" Supper was the one meal the brothers were expected to help clean up.

"Because she's a guest. One day you'll realize there are many perks to bringin' a woman home." Their mother stared Asher down as if she were ready to throttle her most outgoing son.

Micah clapped his hands loudly before he grabbed a handful of dirty plates. "Let's get to it, boys." Their eldest brother had always been one with a rigid backbone, but taking on the role of ranch manager last year after Dad's heart attack had removed any penchant for fun and leniency he might have once possessed.

Noah grabbed Camille's hand to catch her attention. She looked down at their linked fingers and then back up at him with a smile.

"Let's get outta here before she changes her mind or they start protesting."

Camille nodded and followed him out. He slipped on his boots at the edge of the porch. The sun was beginning to set as oranges and purples fought for control of the sky.

Camille stretched her arms above her head and filled her lungs with fresh air. "This place is beautiful."

"You always said that... before."

"I think I'll always say it. There are some beautiful places on this earth, but God spent a lot of time on Wyoming."

Noah could think of a few more beautiful things he was thankful for, like Camille's smile and her generous heart.

"Want to take a walk to my place?" Noah asked. "My truck is parked down there, so I could drive us back."

"I'd love to." She reached for his hand as if it were the natural thing to do. Was she remembering him or was she just growing more comfortable with him? It was dangerous to assume either way.

Dixie bounded up the dirt path, stopping right in front of Noah. He leaned down to scratch her ears and pat her side. "This is Dixie."

"She's beautiful." Camille held out her hands, palms up, and Dixie rested her head in the cradle. Camille moved one hand to rub the black patch that ran from Dixie's nape to cover most of her body. The white on her feet and face was tinted brown from the dry dirt.

"She's a good ranch hand. We got her about four years ago as a pup."

Camille and Noah began walking again, and Dixie traipsed along beside them, occasionally running off to investigate something in the tall grass lining the path.

"What made you decide to move back here for good? I mean, I know you said you didn't want to go back to your old job, but what about Portland?" he asked.

"I couldn't imagine leaving this place. I couldn't remember any friends in Portland, and I knew I wasn't going back to that job." She shrugged. "Why not stay here? I like it here."

Noah liked that answer, and he tried to contain his smile.

Camille nudged his shoulder as she walked beside him. "Tell me a secret."

Noah recalled a conversation they'd had years ago. They'd been teenagers figuring out feelings and the ties that bind people together.

"You wanna know the secret to life?" he asked.

Camille turned to him with one eyebrow cocked. "Always eat dessert first?"

Noah chuckled and shook his head. "Not that one."

"What then?"

Noah quoted the words Camille had once said to him. "You have to follow your heart." He turned to her to gauge her reaction.

Camille stopped walking. To his surprise, she looked at him as if she remembered.

"Even when you're scared." She tilted her head up to him, and creases formed between her brows in confusion. "No, that's the secret of love... I think."

The weight of that one word hung heavy in the

air around them, but it felt more like a blanket than a burden.

She stepped onto a thick fence post lying beside the barn and placed one foot in front of the other to keep her balance. She never released his hand. Walking over the small gap between the wooden beams, her foot slipped where it landed. She tried to right herself, but her body tilted toward him. He released her hand and caught her in his arms before she could fall.

Camille clung to his shirt with one hand, and the other wrapped around the back of his neck. She froze as if she might fall farther if she wiggled.

After a moment to gather her wits, she looked into his eyes. The sun had fallen behind the distant mountains, and shadows covered her face.

Noah's breathing hitched. She was so close. He held her tight and wished he could always keep her here like this.

"I don't remember being clumsy," she whispered as her gaze drifted to his lips.

Did she want him to kiss her? What else did she remember?

"You were always clumsy, but I'm not complaining." Noah could barely breathe. Life didn't get much better than having Camille in his arms.

"Why aren't we together?" she whispered into the twilight.

Noah cleared his throat. "We were for a bit... in Colorado."

"Colorado?" Her brow furrowed with confusion. "You're joking."

"Nope."

"What happened in Colorado?" she asked.

He wanted to tell her everything. So much had happened on that trip, and they'd been the best few days of his life that preceded the worst years. How could he sum it up in a story?

"You'll remember." At least he hoped she would. If she remembered Colorado, maybe everything would come back to her. The crux of their relationship had happened there.

She smiled as if she knew how deeply their proximity affected him. "You gonna put me down, cowboy?"

Noah gathered his wits and placed her on her feet. She reached for his hand and tugged it a little to let him know she wanted to keep walking.

"What happened after Colorado?" she asked sheepishly. "Why aren't we still together?"

And that was the part he hoped to never revisit —the part he couldn't tell her.

He had to give her something, and there was one truth he *could* tell. "We were best friends our whole lives. When our feelings changed, so did our lives."

Noah looked at her and wished he could tell her they could be together without the threat her stepdad had hung on their relationship. "That hasn't changed. There are still reasons why we probably shouldn't be together." He turned away from her. He didn't want to see the disappointment, the hurt on her face.

"It seems like everything has changed. Why not that? Isn't it something we can put behind us?" she asked.

Noah rubbed a hand over his face in frustration. His anger rose as he realized he couldn't just pull Camille into his arms and kiss her the way he wanted to. There were still dangers that kept them apart, and he needed to remember that.

"Let's get one thing straight. The way I feel about you wasn't restricted by time or distance. It changed and grew, and it's still very much there, holding onto the hope I don't have a right to keep."

Camille stepped closer and wrapped her other hand around his arm. It was a comforting gesture. Shouldn't he be comforting her? She was the one battling a world of confusion.

"Where is your place?" she asked quietly.

"Just down there." He pointed toward the slight rise ahead. "I have something I'd like to give you if that's okay."

Camille gave him a smile as if the somber tone of their conversation hadn't bothered her. "Sure. I'm eager to see what you could possibly have for me."

They were quiet as they walked down the hill to

his cabin. The wrangler's quarters were decades old, but he didn't mind. He was a simple man with few needs, and the small cabin suited him just fine.

He pushed open the wooden door and released Camille's hand to turn on the light. He gestured for her to enter first. She hesitantly moved into the space and he followed.

Camille let her gaze fall on every surface. Most of the cabin was exposed from where they stood at the door. "This is nice."

Noah didn't pick up a lie in her voice. He knew when Camille was being genuine. "Thanks. My brothers and I each took one of the old cabins so we could be on site to help. Hunter has one too."

"He's your cousin, right?"

"Right. He works the ranch full-time."

He scratched the back of his neck as Camille moved to the small shelf beside the wood-burning stove.

"What's this?"

She'd found the only photograph in the whole cabin. A moment in time that had captured the two of them, young and happy. Their cheeks were pressed together, and Camille's eyes were closed in laughter.

She picked up the frame and held it gently. "What happened to us?" She didn't look at him as she asked the question he couldn't answer.

Noah moved to her and slowly pulled the picture

from her hand, placing it back on the shelf. Her head tilted up to him, and the look of sadness he saw there tore his chest wide open.

He took both of her hands in his as she faced him. "If you really care, and if you want something to happen between us, just say so. I'll do everything in my power to fix what broke us, but it won't be easy."

He couldn't tell her that her stepdad was the one keeping them apart. Nathan had power that could crush the lives of so many people that Noah cared about, and he'd have to tread lightly. Working around Nathan Vanderbilt's threats wouldn't happen overnight.

Camille nodded. "Yes. I trust you. I know I should. Not because someone told me I used to trust you, but because I can see it in your eyes and hear it in your voice when you talk to me. I'm trying to be patient, but I know it comes at a cost to you. You already know everything."

He pulled her into his chest, and her arms wrapped around his waist. He smelled her hair and wished he could give her everything. That was the hang-up. Wasn't it? That he couldn't live up to the Vanderbilt name and give Camille a life of luxury.

But standing here with her in his meager cabin that she'd accepted, none of that seemed to matter. She was here with him because she'd chosen to be here, and that meant more to him than her last name.

"Trust me. I'll figure this out."

Camille nodded. "I had a dream about you last night. Actually, I think it was a memory."

Noah pulled back to look her in the eye. "Oh, really? Good or bad?"

"I remember being at a creek, and we were lying on a boulder near the bank."

He knew the place. It was their place beside Bluestone Creek where they liked to hide out. They'd been there hundreds of times. She could be thinking about a number of times they'd been together.

"I've had a few memories about that place, actually." She looked up at him and tilted her head. "Are you sure we were just friends all those years?"

Noah bit his lips between his teeth as he decided how to answer. "We were more than friends at one point."

"Right. Colorado."

"Then you left for college."

"And then we broke up?" she asked.

There were facts to fill in, but that was the gist of it. "Yeah."

Camille bit her lip as she took in his words. "Will you still take me there? To the creek that I remembered? I think it was a beautiful place that meant a lot to me."

"Sure. We'll need to go when the sun's out, and

we'll need to take a truck. It's not within walking distance." He wasn't sure if her stepdad would approve of her being here tonight much less coming back to spend time at the pond. Maybe she wasn't telling her parents where she was going. She was a grown woman, after all. "Let's just keep this between us."

"Our secret?" she asked.

"It always was."

Camille tilted her head and narrowed her eyes at him. "Jenny warned me not to talk about you too much to my parents."

"Jenny's a smart woman."

Before she could ask more questions, he pulled her to the small kitchen area. "Here. I said I had something for you." He grabbed the bag from the table and handed it to her.

Camille examined the wad of tissue paper in her hands.

"What is it?" Her face lit up in excitement.

"Open it. I didn't get a chance to wrap it up in something nice." It was still bundled up in the paper his co-worker, Ted, had wrapped it in at Blackwater Restoration earlier.

Camille carefully pulled the vase from the protective paper.

"Noah! It's the vase I said I liked today." She dropped the paper and cradled the gift in her hands, examining it.

Noah smiled. He knew she'd like it. He'd bought it while she was on her lunch break today. He dramatically crooned, "Aww, romantic," as if coaxing her to the reaction.

Camille laughed and threw her head back in ecstasy. "Was that supposed to be my line?"

Noah laughed along with her. "Well, you missed the cue."

She moved the vase to one hand and wrapped her other hand around the back of his neck to pull him in. "I love it."

The words were on the tip of his tongue. If only he could say them right now with the knowledge that no one would get hurt by it later.

I love you.

Instead, he kept his words casual as he tried not to let his mind wander to kissing her. "I'm glad."

Camille looked toward the window. The night was turning darker by the minute. "I think I need to get going."

"We should drive back. Walking around the ranch at night isn't smart."

They drove back to the main house in a comfortable silence, and he parked his old pickup truck beside her SUV.

She turned her whole body to face him in her seat and smiled. The faint light from the windows of the main house cast a glow on the side of her face and hair. "I had fun tonight."

"I did too."

"Good night. I'll see you tomorrow?" she questioned, hopeful.

Tomorrow. He could make that work. "Sure. I'll come pick you up around noon. I need to feed the cows in the morning."

"No need. I'll just meet you here."

Noah shook his head. "I want to pick you up, please." He'd always driven her around when they were younger. Not because he wanted to have the control of driving, but because she hadn't liked driving. He wondered if things were the same now.

"Suit yourself. See you tomorrow."

She jumped from the car without giving him time to think about how much he'd like to kiss her good night.

Fortunately, hearing her say "tomorrow" was the brightest part of his night. There would be more of her to love tomorrow, and that was a wonderful thought.

CHAPTER 12
CAMILLE

That night, Camille tossed and turned. Unable to fall into a restful sleep, she dreamed about Colorado. The scenery and the memories kept flooding her mind.

Their high school graduating class would be taking a trip to Boulder, Colorado in late summer, but Nathan had refused to allow Camille to go. Her studies were too important, and she needed to be focused and ready for college. She would start college in Portland in less than a month.

Camille wanted to go to the resort with her classmates so much that it invaded every moment of her thoughts, but knowing Noah wasn't going either made it more tolerable. Though, she suspected he wasn't going because she wasn't going.

Flashes of pleas and angry words with Nathan crowded her mind. Hurt and anger lingered in her heart, but the dream only revealed a glimpse of the altercation.

Then Noah was there asking her if she wanted to go anyway. They could drive to Boulder for the weekend. He knew some friends who said there was at least one spot in a girl's room and one in a boy's room.

She recalled the slight hesitation to disobey her stepdad, but in the end, her eagerness to go had won out. They'd snuck out after dark and driven through the night. She'd woken up in Boulder the next morning.

Her dream was full of adventures and laughter with Noah and their friends. But most of all, she remembered how he'd been there when the sun went down. She'd cuddled up in his lap by the fire pit where they sat with their friends telling stories and laughing into the night. She could feel the warmth of his chest against one cheek and the heat from the fire against the other. His arms had rested comfortably around her, and she'd known then that nothing would be the same between them again. They were more than friends, and nothing would stop them now.

Then, the dream shifted, and they were standing outside her room at the resort. Noah closed the distance between them, throwing off his baseball cap and pulling her against him in the same moment. When their lips touched, the heat and the power in his kiss rivaled the burn that lingered on her face from the fire.

The kiss ended in her foggy dream, and her mind begged to bring it back. What had it been like? She needed to hang onto it. His arms around her, his lips moving slowly over hers, the fire in his eyes when he pulled away.

Wait, why was he pulling away? Why was he fading like a ghost in the fog?

Then Nathan appeared again. This time, he was yelling. His face was red, and the veins in his neck protruded unnaturally.

Camille woke panting and covered in sweat. The rush of the dream lingered, and her heart beat too fast. She placed her hand on her chest as if she could settle the rhythm.

How much of the dream had been her memory, and how much had been just that... a dream?

She gulped water from the bottle beside her bed, and then rested back against the pillows. Closing her eyes, she tried to make sense of it all.

She was sure she and Noah had gone to Colorado. He'd told her so. Was that how it had happened? She could imagine Nathan would've been furious if she'd gone behind his back and snuck off like that.

What had she been thinking?

She'd been thinking about a weekend away with Noah, and she'd had it, according to her dream. Forcing her breaths to calm, she searched her brain for anything else she could remember about the trip.

A vision of Noah driving his truck along an open highway flashed in her mind, and she remembered being cuddled up beside him trailing innocent kisses on his neck.

"Stop it, Millie," he'd protested feebly.

Then he'd stopped for gas, and she remembered how he'd seized her lips in a hard kiss that she recalled all too well.

Her brows scrunched together, and she closed her eyes tighter trying to think of what he'd said next.

"Listen, Millie. Nathan is going to lose it when we get back. If we make it out of this alive, I want you to know I don't regret it. I wouldn't change a thing."

Camille's heart sank to her toes, and she covered her mouth to hush the sob threatening to escape. So much more than memories were coming back to her now. She knew she cared about Noah Harding more than anyone had let on in these last six months of her recovery, and the realization that Nathan could be the one keeping them apart had her blood running cold.

CHAPTER 13
NOAH

Noah usually liked working with Aaron. His steadfast brother was more interested in staying the course and getting the work finished. He needed to get back to the main house where their mom watched Levi while whey worked. Aaron wasn't one to chat about the weather or complain about the slow calving season. He kept his head down and finished the work.

Today, Aaron kept cutting glances his way. To be fair, it might have had something to do with the force Noah had chucked the bales as they loaded the hay pens.

"Anything you wanna get off your chest?" Aaron finally asked.

Noah jumped from the bed of the truck and removed his gloves before cutting the ties on a square bale. "It's Camille."

"I figured as much, but I don't have anything for you when it comes to women." Aaron had been raising his son alone since his ex left two and a half years ago without looking back. She hadn't been one to be tied down to a ranch.

"What's the holdup?" Aaron asked. "Things seem to be goin' okay. Just go for it."

"They would be, if Nathan Vanderbilt wasn't dead set against me."

"So what if the guy doesn't like you? Camille is a grown woman. She can date whoever she wants."

Noah shook his head. Maybe Aaron had a right to know. It would be his job on the line if Noah couldn't figure out a way to get Nathan off his back. Aaron had the most to lose since he had to provide for his kid.

Noah turned to his brother and rested his arm on the side of the hay truck. "He told me if I didn't leave her alone that he'd sink the ranch. At the hospital when she got hurt six months ago, he told me the deal still stands. I let her go to protect the family."

"What do you mean by sink the ranch?" Aaron asked, keenly intent on the conversation now.

"I mean, he said he'd make sure every Harding was out of a job. We all live here. As if we needed another outside factor that could ruin any given season, Nathan has the power to destroy the entire ranch."

The color left Aaron's face, and he rubbed the stubble on his cheek. "He can't do that." His voice was full of fear.

Noah went on, driving the threat home. "You remember when Nathan had the brewery in town shut down because he was opening his own down the street? And what about Harrison's Pharmacy? His friend owned a rival store, so he uncovered a handful of alleged charges of illegal distribution."

Aaron's face was turning a sickly green. "I get it."

Noah was on a roll now, sinking further and further into his anger. "Do you?" he asked with a sneer. Noah ticked off another local business with his finger. "What about JoJo's Diner?"

"I get it!" Aaron shouted. The few cows that had already made it to the feeding pen skittered back a few feet. "Sheesh, you're right. If there's bad blood between you and Nathan Vanderbilt, you're outta luck."

"Micah is the only one who knows the story," Noah confessed. "I figured he was the only one who really needed to know, runnin' the ranch and all. He needed to be prepared. Nathan has had his thumb over us for years. What would happen if he killed our herds? What about another fire? He could cut off our water or cut the ties we have with suppliers."

"Can we stop playing what if?" Aaron asked as he spread the hay across the opening. "What did

Micah say about it? He's smart about this kinda stuff."

"He thinks a woman isn't worth puttin' a dozen people out of a job, but he'd never say as much. He didn't have to back then because I let her go." And he hadn't fought for her. The realization still left a sour taste in his mouth.

"Smart man," Aaron mumbled. "We can't let Nathan sink his teeth in here. There's too much at stake."

"Listen, I know." Noah rubbed the back of his neck. "I don't want Dad finding out about this. He doesn't need the stress. I won't let anything happen to the ranch."

"I sure hope you know what you're doing. We've got all our eggs in one basket here."

"I understand."

Noah wasn't sure what he was doing yet. He'd been praying, but the Lord hadn't gifted him a clear path. There weren't many people he could talk to about the situation.

He pulled his gloves out of his back pocket and put them on as he hopped back into the bed of the truck. Aaron slid into the driver's seat and drove them to the next hay pen without a word.

Noah pulled up to Camille's house at noon. She'd given him her address the night before. She burst from the door and was running to greet him before he had a chance to get out of the truck. "Hey, stranger!"

"Hey yourself. Ready to remember?" he asked.

She bounded over to the passenger side and jumped in before he even made it around the side of the truck. "You bet. Let's get a move on."

Noah walked back to the driver's side with a grin on his face. They rode in silence for a few minutes before the wailing of an ambulance siren split the quiet. The emergency vehicle raced past them, and Noah looked at Camille to find her head down and her eyes closed.

When she opened her eyes and found him looking at her, she jumped. "For Pete's sake, Noah. You scared me."

"Why?"

"I was just..."

"Praying?" he asked.

"How did you know?"

Noah shook his head. "You're the only person I know who prays in the moment." He reached for her hand, and she squeezed his back. "When someone asks you to pray for them, you do it right then and there. You used to always pray when you heard an ambulance siren. You said it meant someone needed help."

"I still do that," she whispered.

"Because you're good down to your bones, Millie."

Camille tilted her head to look at him. "Millie?"

"Oh, do you not like that name? I used to call you that sometimes."

"I like it. It's just that I had a dream last night and you called me that."

Noah waited for her to say more about the dream. He didn't want to coax her all the time. She'd tell him when she was ready.

"Yeah, I had a dream about Colorado. I blame you for mentioning it yesterday."

Noah's blood pressure rose. If she remembered Colorado, she knew everything that mattered. "And?" He couldn't help the question this time.

"And there's a lot about us that I didn't know before. Some that I'm still not sure about." She laid her other hand over their clasped hands. "I wish I'd known sooner... about Colorado."

Noah nodded. "Yeah, me too."

He'd loved Camille quietly for years, like snowflakes drifting down and settling on branches. Now, he loved her fiercely like the destructive weather at the changing of seasons.

If only he could tell her.

CHAPTER 14
CAMILLE

Camille stepped from the truck and studied the scene around her. The warm June air brushed the skin of her arms in the breeze, and the water was bubbling quietly in the deep blue creek.

"I do remember this place. It's Bluestone Creek."

Noah rounded the truck and halted. "You remembered the name?" Noah asked.

"Yeah, sometimes I can associate a name with a person or place. I don't think there's a rhyme or reason to the names that I remember." She shrugged.

They made their way to the bank and she dipped to her knees. Raking her fingers through the brisk water, she had the urge to jump in.

"Did we swim here?" she asked.

"Once, accidentally. The water stays cool."

"But we did?"

"We did."

"What else did we do around here?"

He moved close and squatted beside her. "Back then, you were interested in anything outdoors. You tried to name the cows, but there were too many. You'd get frustrated when we had to move the herds and you'd lose track of the ones you'd befriended."

She laughed. "What about the horses?"

"You always loved the horses. There was one that you claimed as your own. It was Mom's, but she hardly ever rode it."

Camille grinned. "Skye."

"Yeah."

"I guess she isn't around anymore?" The horse could have still been here, but she'd picked up on the *was* he'd used when talking about the horse.

"We lost her a few years ago."

The quiet fell around them, and Camille stood. Noah rose to his feet beside her and placed a hand on her arm.

"Hey, it's all right. She didn't suffer. Lucas handles the horses around here, and he can help you pick out another one."

Camille sucked in a deep breath and nodded. "Yeah. I'd like that. I don't remember much about riding horses, but I'm gonna hope it's like riding a bike."

Noah laughed and pulled her by the hand downriver. She could see the boulder from her memories just beyond the bend.

"That's it," she said when she spotted it.

"That's it," Noah admitted. "We came here for the first time when we were fourteen. You asked me to take you somewhere special. I had a truck, but I didn't have the money to take you out someplace nice or anything, so I brought you here."

"Let me guess. I loved it."

"You loved it. You always wanted to come back here, too. You said it was just the two of us here."

The phone rang in Camille's pocket, but she didn't reach for it. Noah looked at her, expecting she would answer.

"Just let that ring."

"What if it's important?" Noah asked.

"It's not."

She was almost sure it was her mom, and they'd already spoken three times today. Her mother was calling more often than usual, and Camille could only wonder if Nathan was pushing the conversations. Her mom always asked questions about where she was or where she'd been and who she'd been with, and Camille couldn't remember her mom being like that before. In fact, she hadn't been quite so nosy even after her injury.

They reached the large boulder that was big enough for both of them to climb up on and lay at an angle facing the creek. Camille laid one hand on the rock to pull herself up when her phone rang again.

The phone calls were dampening the mood of her afternoon with Noah.

"Hold on."

She declined the call knowing she couldn't answer it right now anyway. Her mother would ask her where she was, and Camille wasn't ready to tell her she was with Noah. Jenny and Noah had both advised her against it.

"I think I need to go. Maybe we can come back some other time?" she asked, praying he'd say yes.

"Any time," he said. "I understand."

"Things are just... fragile between my mom and me right now. I don't know how to tell her she's smothering me."

Noah held up his hands in surrender. "I don't have the answers there. I know Bonnie was always good to me, but she cares about you a lot. You were her miracle baby, and your parents knew they wouldn't have any other kids. So when she lost your dad when you were young, she clung to you a little tighter."

Camille was sure he was repeating the things she'd once told him, but it put her mom's recent behavior change into perspective and softened her frustrations with the constant calls.

"I think you're right."

Maybe she was reading too much into things by

thinking Nathan was behind everything. Sure, she had an inkling that he might have something to do with Noah's distance, but she didn't have any proof. Until then, maybe she just needed to keep her head down and listen.

CHAPTER 15
NOAH

It was the second day of his shift with the fire department, and Noah was lounging in the rec room, while the other men in his crew lazily chatted around him. His eyes were drifting closed, but he wasn't contributing anything groundbreaking to the conversation anyway. He doubted anyone would notice if he fell asleep.

Lucas plopped down in the other reclining chair in the sectional sofa and made an exaggerated huff. "Dude, what are you doing?"

"What does it look like," Noah said. "I'm watching the back of my eyelids."

Lucas shoved Noah's shoulder. "Come on. I need someone to watch *Live PD* with me. It's not as fun if I'm the only one in the peanut gallery."

Noah pried his eyes open and sat up. "How do you function on so little sleep?"

"I just don't need that much of a reboot. I'm hardwired for fun."

The call sounded, and everyone in the room groaned. The entire crew was reaching their limit.

Lucas stood and stalked to the kitchen area. "I didn't even get to eat my sandwich." He threw the peanut butter and jelly sandwich into the trash before whirling his finger in the air. "Round 'em up, gentlemen."

Noah listened to the dispatch and noted a burning chemical smell at an office building downtown. The ambulance might not be needed, but they loaded up out of an abundance of caution.

About halfway there, he realized they were headed to the office building where Camille's stepdad's practice was located. There was a chance he wouldn't see Nathan, but the thought of running into him after Noah had been spending so much time with Camille recently was enough to have him sweating in his uniform.

The building had been evacuated before they arrived, and since no one needed medical attention, Noah searched the building for others. When he arrived back at the entrance, his crew had located the source of the smell and the wiring issue that needed to be addressed.

Once the threat was clear, Noah made his way back to the engine on autopilot. Hopefully, the home stretch of this shift would be a quiet one.

Before he reached the engine, Nathan stepped into his path. Disheveled and tired, Noah looked much less than his best.

"Mr. Harding, I didn't expect to see you here." Nathan's pride balanced unwavering on his upturned nose.

"Just responding to the call, sir."

Nathan's demeanor was calm as he said, "I trust you're keeping your word."

Noah rubbed his face in frustration. "Listen, I didn't push back when you told me I couldn't see her in the hospital, but this is crossing a line. I haven't done anything wrong."

"You don't have to," Nathan explained. "The only thing you need to worry about is keeping your distance. Camille has a serious injury, but she can still practice law. I want her focused on getting back into the office."

"In Oregon?" Noah asked.

Nathan smiled. "You kept up with her. I don't know if you're smart or stupid."

Noah's chest rose and fell like the hills and valleys of a roller coaster. "I haven't done anything wrong," Noah repeated.

Nathan's gaze slid down Noah's uniform and back up and he said, "We'll see," before walking off.

Noah didn't say a word on the way back to the station. Once he was out of his uniform, he closed himself in his room and vowed to sleep. Too bad the anger in his head was loud enough to keep him awake.

Hours later, Lucas stepped into the double room they shared. "What are you doing sitting in the dark?"

"I can't sleep." Noah sat on the side of his bunk with his head in his hands.

"I saw you with Nathan earlier. What's his deal?"

"He doesn't want me and Camille to be together, so he's threatening me. It's been going on for years."

"What? That's ridiculous. You and Camille are like a sure thing. What's his issue?"

"She's a Vanderbilt. I'm a Harding. Might as well be a Montague and a Capulet."

Lucas's face scrunched to one side. "Like that Leonardo DiCaprio movie from the nineties?"

Noah laughed. "Yeah, like that. Nathan wants her to marry someone from their social circle, not mine."

"Well, he'll get over it," Lucas said.

"No, he won't." Noah stood and paced in the small room. "His threats are real. At least, I believe him. He has the clout to make anything happen."

"Okay, so make him like you."

"I wish I could, but I'm all out of winning lottery tickets. I'd need money—something I don't have."

"No, make him like *you*. Be a gentleman and

have a man-to-man talk with him. Mind your P's and Q's and maybe bring him a gift."

"I'm not trying to date *him*," Noah reminded his brother. "He doesn't like the fact that I'm a cowboy, and that's not something I could change. Well, I *could* leave, but then I'd just be down a job and the ranch would be down a worker."

Lucas knocked his knuckles against the wooden frame of the bunk beds. "Well, at least pray about it. And it wouldn't hurt to practice a speech or something. I know talking isn't your thing, but you could Google it."

Noah grinned. His brother had lightened his mood while still managing to annoy him. "Thanks, I'll keep that in mind."

CHAPTER 16
CAMILLE

Camille smiled when she heard the bell above the door ring. She knew it would be Noah when she scooted her chair back from the desk in her office. It was the day he volunteered, and she hadn't seen him since he'd taken her to Bluestone Creek, though they'd talked on the phone daily.

Noah was already approaching the checkout counter as she stepped from her office. His hair was damp from a shower, and his white T-shirt hugged his shoulders just right. How did he always look so good? She narrowed her eyes at him as he approached with too much swagger. It was too early for her stomach to be doing flips over a good lookin' man.

He smiled and locked his arms to lean on the counter. "What's got you in a huff?"

She just looked at him, daring him to be more handsome than he already was.

When she didn't answer, he continued.

"You're cute when you're mad."

"You're too cute for your own good." If he wasn't so handsome and charming, she might have been over him years ago. "It's frustrating that I want to kiss you just because you walk into the room."

Shock registered in Noah's features. Her boldness wasn't something new, but it was with him. At least, since her injury.

His grin grew, and she couldn't take her eyes off his straight teeth.

"You're welcome." His deep voice held a timbre she felt in her middle.

Yep, frustratingly handsome.

The beginnings of a headache pounded over her temple, and she rubbed the spot to dispel the ache.

"How are you feeling? Headache?" he asked.

Camille had hoped the headaches would've eased up by now, but they had decided to keep their steady course.

"It's nothing. Just a headache. I get them sometimes."

The neurologist had said they were nothing to be concerned about. That didn't mean they weren't a pain in her behind.

"I know the recovery has been slow, but you're

doing great. Every day is one step farther from your injury."

She hadn't been thinking about it that way, but he was right.

Noah leaned in and whispered, "Just remember, you're extraordinary even on a bad day." He stepped away and went to work in the delivery bay with Ted, leaving her breathless.

Did he know what it meant to her when he said things like that? He was filling in the pieces of the puzzle of her life with patience, but he was also reminding her that it was okay to take her time. That independence she was fighting for was within reach when he came around building her up like that.

The store had been busy with deliveries the last few days, and Noah had his work cut out for him with the backlog of furniture to be moved. At noon, he knocked on her open office door and propped against the doorframe.

"Hey, handsome," she greeted him, looking up from her computer.

She'd need to ask Kathy about the company dating policy. Although, technically, Noah wasn't an employee or a contract worker. He was a volunteer, which meant a relationship between them should be safe. At least, she wanted it to be—if he'd ever ask her on a real date or say something to make things official.

His white T-shirt collected splotches of moisture, and his hair was sweaty. How did he still look so good?

Noah tilted his head at her compliment and said, "Would you like to go to Barn Sour with me tonight?"

"You mean the place with the live music and dancing?" she questioned.

"Yeah, that one."

"I'd love it, but I don't know how to dance."

Noah chuckled and shook his head. "Yeah, you do. It's like riding a bike."

He winked at her, and her heart skipped a beat. She was sure of it. Palpitations were happening.

"I'll pick you up at six if that's okay."

Camille nodded, too unsure of her voice to speak.

Noah pushed his shoulder off the doorframe, backing out of the office, with his gaze locked on her until he was out of sight.

When she was alone again, she squealed and did a little happy dance. She'd finally gotten a date with Noah Harding.

———

Camille rushed home and jumped in the shower. When she was standing in front of her closet, she called Jenny.

"Hello."

"Jen, what do I wear dancing?" Camille asked as if the answer should be given rapid-fire style.

"Um, a dress?" Jenny offered.

"Good call. What kinda dress?"

"A pretty one. Are you going on a date with Noah?" Jenny's excitement grew with her pitch. "Where are you going?"

"You bet! That man could have asked me to go muck out the stalls, and I'd have said yes. He's taking me to Barn Sour."

Jenny laughed. "Good. That place is out in the middle of nowhere. I bet you were eager for him to ask. The two of you are made for each other."

"I think so too," Camille agreed.

Jenny's voice dipped to a serious level. "I'm really happy for you, Millie. I always hoped you'd be this happy again, and I figured it wouldn't happen with anyone but him."

"Why do I hear a 'but' coming?"

"Just be careful."

"You don't think he'll hurt me, do you?" Camille was referring to her heart. She knew that was the only thing at risk of being damaged in this relationship.

"I don't. Not if he can help it."

CHAPTER 17
CAMILLE

Camille held Noah's hand as they walked into Barn Sour, or just "The Barn" as most people called it. The rustic restaurant and bar was popular with the country locals, and the place was already packed on a Friday night. She'd taken Jenny's suggestion and opted for a lightweight dress with cap sleeves. Noah looked handsome in a navy and gray pearl snap shirt with the sleeves rolled up to his elbows.

The band on the stage tweaked their equipment as Noah leaned in close to her ear to be heard above the noise. When his breath tickled her ear, she giggled.

"Let's sit there." He pointed to an empty booth in the back of the main room.

She nodded and followed him, holding his hand

as they wound their way through the milling patrons.

They leaned in close over the table to hear each other above the sound of the band while they waited for their food. She ordered the tater totchos at Noah's recommendation, and she found herself impressed when they arrived.

"You're right. This is delicious. I could eat my weight in these."

Noah smiled and took another bite of his Reuben. "Just wait until you try the bread pudding."

"You spoil me."

Noah winked at her. "Just want my date to leave here happy."

Oh, she thought that would be easy.

When the waitress took their empty dishes, Camille looked over to the dance floor. The people moved across the open space like bees in a hive. Everyone knew their place. One wrong move and dancers would be falling on their behinds.

Noah stood and extended his hand to her, palm up. "Wanna dance?"

"I really don't remember how to dance."

"That's okay. You will. Let me lead."

She took his hand, and a sense of calm came over her as she followed him to the floor.

They began with a two-step that he walked her through until she got the hang of it. Soon, she was moving with more confidence and laughing at herself when she missed a step.

The next song was a country swing dance. Should she bow out of this one?

Noah wouldn't let her. Instead, he pulled her in close and coached her through each move. Soon, the movements were coming back to her, and she was having fun. By the fifth dance, she had it down pat, and breathlessly danced as if her life depended on it. The moves were as effortless as if she'd done them her whole life. How many times had they done this together in the past?

The upbeat, lively dances were her favorite. Every move that sent her dancing away from him would inevitably bring her back. The certainty of it was comforting, and she liked being cradled in his arms, if only for a few seconds.

At the end of a song, he pulled her in close and held her still. The rush of the dance was thrilling, and she felt a little reckless. The band announced their short break, but she didn't move from the safety of Noah's arms.

"Apparently, my muscle memory is quicker to remember than I thought."

Noah didn't speak. His face held a serious expression, and she wondered if he'd kiss her. She didn't care if dozens of people were watching.

She looked up into his eyes, begging him to kiss

her the way she dreamed he had in Colorado. "You think a kiss would spark a memory?" she asked.

Noah's nostrils flared as he sucked in a deep breath and set his jaw. "A kiss would tell you a lot."

His breathing evened, and his smirk grew into something mischievous. He was daring her to do it, but could she? She especially wanted to remember how his lips felt against hers.

Someone shoved her back, and she fell forward into Noah, causing his footsteps to falter.

"Hey!" Noah's deep voice boomed above the noisy people. "Watch where you're pushin'."

A rotund man with a sweaty face squared up to Noah.

"I'll push wherever I want." He pointed at Camille as he moved closer into Noah's space. "You need to keep your woman outta my way."

Oh no. It was clear the man was well on his way to being drunk, and he didn't seem to care who he'd knocked over.

"Hey, um, let's just go. It's fine." Camille tugged on Noah's arm, but he was rooted to the ground.

"I think you owe my girlfriend an apology," Noah countered, stepping up to meet the man match for match.

The man's friend was already pushing him back and apologizing on his behalf when the drunk man shoved Noah purposely.

"No way!" the drunk man roared.

Noah stepped toward the man, and Camille yelled, "Noah!" as she tugged harder on his arm, trying to keep him back.

He stopped, his feet stuck to the ground as if concrete had dried around them. A woman barged onto the scene and started pushing them apart.

"Back it up, fellas! I'll show you both out."

"He started it." The sweaty man pointed at Noah.

But the woman's eyes were on the troublemaker as her shoulders squared.

"Listen here, Tommy, I *know* it was you. I ain't even gotta ask the witnesses. I already know you'll be outta here early. It ain't even eight thirty. Come on!" She sounded exasperated.

Noah turned to Camille with a look of apology. He'd stopped on a dime when she'd called his name, but he'd been ready to defend her until she'd spoken up.

He took a deep breath, and then another. "I'm sorry. I just... I didn't like him pushing you."

"I know, but it isn't worth a fight, and that guy looked ready to split some heads."

"I'm ashamed to say I was too." Noah stretched his hands out wide, then relaxed them. "Sorry. You're right. I shouldn't have gotten worked up like that."

Camille jerked her head toward the door. He'd already settled the bill before they started dancing. "Come on. Let's go. I could use a drive."

CHAPTER 18
NOAH

When the fog cleared from his mind, Noah remembered the anger and the red he'd seen when that guy had pushed Camille. Her voice had caught hold of him and pulled him out of his stampede. In that moment, he hadn't been in control of his own body. But then Camille called to him, and he'd bent to her command.

It didn't bother him. He'd needed to be called out of that cloud of anger. Sometimes, she had to be the level-headed one.

The Barn was one place he could take Camille out in public without the fear of Nathan or someone he knew spotting them and getting word back to her stepdad. The company Nathan kept wouldn't be caught dead in a place like Barn Sour, but starting a fight in a public place might draw undesired attention from the locals. The last thing he wanted right now was for his name to be connected to Camille's in gossip circles.

"Where do you wanna go?" he asked as he opened the passenger door of his truck for her to step in.

"Can we go to the ranch for a bit? I know it's getting late, but I don't have anywhere to be tomorrow."

"The ranch it is." He closed her door and walked around to slip into the driver's side.

She was quiet as they drove along the backroads of Blackwater. He slowed their speed, and she stuck her arm out the window. The wind carried her ponytail, and she closed her eyes as she rested her head on her extended arm.

At the ranch, he parked in front of his cabin. When she got out of the truck, she headed toward the stable instead. The horse barn was only about fifty yards from his cabin, but he grabbed a pistol from his truck and shoved it in his ankle holster just to be safe. He was usually cautious on the ranch, but he wasn't taking any chances while Camille was in his care. She jerked her head in the direction she was headed, and he caught up with her to grab her hand.

They walked in silence to the stable. Only the rhythmic crunch of the loose gravel beneath their feet filled the night. He turned to her, and he caught a grin on her face in the dim moonlight.

He opened the stable doors, and she looked both

ways as if they were sneaking around. How did she make everything into an adventure? They were adults on his family ranch, and they had free rein to go most anywhere they pleased, but her mischievous tendencies ran high.

The faint nightlights Lucas had installed cast a dim glow throughout the stables, and Camille stood on her toes to peek into a nearby stall. When she found it empty, she moved to the next one. She moved down the stalls, peeking in each one without commenting until she came to the end.

Noah knew Lucas had brought in a few of the horses tonight so they'd be easier to saddle in the morning for the herding, but what was Camille looking for?

"I just wanted to make sure everyone was sleeping."

Noah laughed. "Why do they need to be sleeping?"

She swished her hips and her ponytail as she walked. The skirt of her dress fanned out around her as she sauntered toward him. When she stopped right in front of him, she grinned and whispered, "I wanted to remind you about that kiss we were talking about earlier."

He didn't need to be reminded. The thought of kissing her hadn't left his mind in weeks. Noah held in a chuckle as he wrapped his arms around her waist and pulled her in close to whisper in her ear.

"And the horses couldn't overhear our scandalous talk of kissing?"

"Right," she breathed.

"You can kiss me if you want to, Millie, but not because you want to remember. If you kiss me, make sure it's for me, not the boy I was."

He leaned back to look her in the eye. He wanted to see if her nerve would hold. Daring her with his gaze, he waited.

She hesitated, but then her arms wrapped tighter around his neck. She leaned in but still didn't close the distance between them.

When he thought his heart would beat straight out of his chest, he said, "If you don't, I will."

Camille grinned and nodded.

Then he kissed her.

Pulling her in close, he felt the emptiness between them dissolve and fill with all the emotion built up over the past weeks. Her mouth moved like water against his, and her fingers dug into his shoulders.

The kiss said just as much about how he felt about her now as it did about how much he'd missed her all those years. From the way she clung to him, he knew she was saying the same thing. He knew she remembered. She knew enough to know that nothing he felt for her had ever been tempered. It had once burned hot and fast, but now it held on like a slow, controlled burn.

When they separated, her fingertips touched her lips and she whispered, "Friends don't kiss like that."

Noah shook his head. "We *were* friends, but there was so much more for a long time before we ever admitted it. You mean so much more to me than just a friend."

Camille pulled him close. "I know. I remember a lot more now, and I can't just act like it didn't happen. I can't pretend I didn't feel something for you back then, and I won't act like there isn't even more now."

Those were the words he'd always dreamed of hearing, but he had to know what she knew about the end of what they'd once shared. He nudged her, and she raised her head.

"Do you remember what happened?"

Camille shook her head. "I remember you pushing me away, but not why." She tilted her head and asked, "What happened?"

He cupped her face. "I want to tell you, but trust me, you don't want to know."

Camille shook her head in his hands.

"Don't say it. I don't wanna know. Not yet. I know I asked, but just... forget I said it."

She'd always been a believer in affirmations. The things we said became the truth, and she'd said some things that made him think she might be onto the truth.

There were moments that asked questions and moments meant for answers.

She brushed a stray hair from his face and let her fingers slide down his cheek. "Now, tell me about these horses. I want to ride with you soon."

He tugged her hand and led her to the first stall. "This is Carson. He's a Quarter Horse we got last year from Georgia."

Moving from stall to stall, he told her about every horse and their unique personalities before promising she could ride a few sometime.

Camille believed everything would be all right, as long as they had each other, and Noah knew they could handle anything with her by his side. But he was on his own when it came to fixing things with her stepdad.

CHAPTER 19
CAMILLE

Camille's phone rang on the nightstand beside her bed, startling her from a sound sleep. She lifted her head and squinted into the dark bedroom. The phone continued to ring, but her tired brain hadn't processed anything beyond the intrusion.

Propping up onto her elbow, she leaned over to look at the glowing phone. It was midnight on the dot, and the caller ID read Noah over a photo of him she'd secretly snapped at Blackwater Restoration. He was wearing a sweaty T-shirt and facing away from her with his hands propped on his hips during a break. She hadn't been able to resist the shameless photo of his backside, and he'd rolled his eyes when she'd shown him later that day.

A knock sounded on her window, and her heart stood at attention. What was outside?

Camille snatched the phone up and answered before it stopped ringing. "Hey."

"Hey, yourself. Come to the window."

Why was he whispering?

She kicked the blankets and sheets from her legs and plodded across the cool floor to her bedroom window. Noah was standing in her backyard holding a phone to his ear.

She raised the window with her free hand and elbow. "What are you doing here?" she asked, still holding the phone to her ear. She could barely make out his facial features from the single streetlight nearby.

"I come bearing gifts," he said, as if it were the most normal thing to show up at her window at midnight.

"What for?"

"Your birthday. Get dressed. We have plans."

Camille's eyebrows shot up, and he laughed quietly before she had time to wonder if he could see her face in the dark. "We had a midnight rendezvous planned? Why isn't it on my calendar?"

"It is. It's your birthday."

She stared at him, still holding the phone to her ear, as if his words didn't make sense.

Noah continued. "It's officially June 29th. Happy birthday."

Midnight. He'd come to her at midnight to be

the first person to wish her a happy birthday. She hadn't even thought about her birthday until now, but he'd remembered.

A grin covered her face. "What did you bring me?"

"It's in the truck. Get dressed and come on." He dropped the phone from his ear and shook his head. They'd been standing three feet apart at the window, so the phones hadn't been necessary.

Camille padded to the bathroom and threw on a dirty pair of jeans and a T-shirt with a huge squirrel on it. She tried her best to make the messy bun she'd slept in into a stylish ponytail, then grabbed her phone and purse and climbed out the window.

Noah was leaning against the side of his truck with his ankles and arms crossed when she snuck quietly through the yard to meet him. "Did you just sneak out the window of your own house?"

Camille wasn't a strict rule follower, but she paid attention to the ones that mattered. That didn't mean it wasn't a little thrilling to *act* like she was being mischievous. "Did you knock on my window instead of my front door?"

Noah's lips formed a thin line as he considered. "Fair enough. Get in."

She slipped into the old pickup and found a plastic container of six vanilla cupcakes with white icing and sprinkles next to a red box that could've fit over the palm of her hand. "For me?" she asked excitedly.

"For you, but wait until we get there."

"Where is there?"

"The creek."

He was taking her to the ranch tonight? She'd get out of bed anytime for that.

"We used to do this every year on your birthday."

All the memories came rushing back to her in an instant. "You're right! I knew that!" Her excitement grew with her volume. "Except that one time it stormed."

"Yep. But we had a rain check."

That had been her sixteenth birthday. The next week, he'd taken her to the creek during the day, along with the traditional cupcakes, and they'd gone swimming. How could she forget that? Nothing had mattered to her back then as much as Noah, and she'd been addicted to the way her heart felt as if it were jumping for joy when he looked at her.

"I remember," she whispered.

He'd been sneaking her out of her parents' house for years. No wonder she'd crawled out the window tonight without thinking twice.

Noah reached across the cab of the truck and took her hand in his as he straightened the truck onto the main road leading to the ranch. "I was hoping you would."

He drove across the ranch to the creek and parked. "Grab the cupcakes." He picked up the small box and jumped out to grab a shotgun from the bed.

Even she knew better than to wander the ranch —night or day—without protection.

She cradled the cupcakes under her arm and remembered why they'd settled on cupcakes all those years ago. Mama Harding's oatmeal raisin cookies were Camille's favorite, but Noah had said his mom would be making those for her birthday anyway, so they needed to take advantage of another sweet and tasty option.

Camille walked beside Noah and wrapped her arm around his. Stepping through tall grass, she was glad she'd thrown on her boots instead of sandals.

The anticipation was bubbling up inside her as she climbed onto the boulder, taking extra precaution not to drop the cupcakes. She settled herself onto the flatter part of the big rock as Noah climbed up, leaving the shotgun propped against the base.

"What now?"

Noah shrugged. "Well, we used to talk about what we thought the next year would be like while we ate the cupcakes."

"Oh, yes," she recalled. "These are yummy cupcakes."

She reached to open the container, but Noah swatted her hand away.

"Not so fast, Cookie Monster. I have another gift this year."

Camille gave a small squeal. "Okay."

She clenched her fists and ground her teeth together to ward off her eagerness. Noah handed her the box, and she removed the lid. A gold heart slid along a thin chain.

"Noah, it's beautiful." She gently touched the heart with the tip of her finger. "It's a locket."

The design was simple. It was a piece she could wear every day. It was something she would've picked for herself because she wasn't flashy or gaudy.

"Thank you. I love it so much." She reached up to touch his cheek, and the stubble pricked her fingers.

"There is something you do need to know," Noah said. "I love you, Camille. I always have, and I always will."

Camille smiled big enough to light up the night and cradled his face in her hands. She'd known her own heart, and she'd guessed that he was feeling the same.

"I love you too."

Those words felt so true and real between them. They had only been together again for a month, but the other years were slowly filling in the gaps for her.

"I love you, Millie. Happy birthday."

His sentiment was overwhelming, and she fought back a happy tear.

Noah leaned in close, and she could smell his cologne. She remembered that scent. He hadn't been wearing it recently, but it was a smell she remembered from before the injury. Smells and sounds seemed to be the most influential in recovering her memories.

"I'm glad your birthday fell on my off day. Sometimes the rotating schedule means I miss out on things like this."

"That's okay if you have to. I'll understand. But tonight, I'm grateful we're here together."

The midsummer moon was nearly full, and she could see the intensity of Noah's gaze.

"I'm grateful we're here together too. Do you know how long I've prayed for this?"

She could only nod her understanding.

"I can't tell you what it means to have you back." He ran a hand up her arm and let it come to rest on the back of her neck. "You've never looked down on me like you could have. You have a heart of gold, and that's one of the many things I love about you."

A heart of gold. The necklace.

"I would never look down on you. You're too important to me. I knew that then, and I know it now."

Noah's hand on the back of her neck tightened, and she leaned in just as he pulled her close. Their lips met perfectly, and she breathed in the crisp air. Something wonderful filled her lungs and spread throughout her body—a warmth and comfort that came from connecting with the one who filled her up, made her stronger, and loved her with the fire of a thousand blazing suns.

When the kiss ended, she was left smiling. "So, tell me something I don't know."

Anything would do, and there were so many things she was aching to know.

Noah thought for a moment. She watched as he tilted his head toward the sky as if looking for answers amidst the stars.

He turned to her, and his face was hidden in shadow. "Do you know why it's called Blackwater Ranch?"

"I don't recall that memory, but should I know?" she asked.

"I think you might have heard it at one point. It was a story my grandpa used to tell me and my brothers when we were young."

Noah leaned back on the rock and propped himself up on his elbows. Camille stayed sitting, but she turned her body toward him to watch him while he spoke.

"My great-great-grandfather, Bennett Harding, started this ranch. No one else wanted the land around Blackwater Creek. There were stories that the water was poison and that the people and animals who settled along the creek died mysteriously.

"But Bennett Harding wasn't convinced. I've heard he was skeptical and cunning, and he wondered why a water source would scare people off. So he packed up the things he needed and set up a shelter where Blackwater Creek intersects Bluestone Creek."

Camille pointed to the nearby water. "This creek?"

"Yeah, it joins Blackwater about a quarter of a mile that way." Noah pointed over her head into the dark night.

Settling back onto his elbows, he continued. "He didn't tell anyone where he was going or what he was doing, but he lived there for a month. He fished in the creek, lived off the land, and he wasn't poisoned. He certainly didn't die. After that, he knew the rumors weren't true. He figured it was the name. With a name like Blackwater, people were bound to get a little suspicious.

"Anyway, he bought the land, and Blackwater has been good to us ever since. We're not one of the bigger ranches around here, but we've done pretty well." Noah shrugged. "Good enough for us Hardings, anyway. We don't need much."

Camille grinned. That was one thing she admired about Noah. He wasn't a man who got caught up in material things. She was the same way in some aspects. She didn't purchase frivolously, and she didn't live outside of her means. The house she'd rented in town was small, but she could've afforded something much larger, even after paying the copious medical bills from her wreck. She'd made big money while working for Parker and Lions.

"Thanks for telling me. I like knowing the history of this place."

"What else do you want to know?" He reached up and touched the end of her ponytail.

She lay down on her side and propped up on one arm, facing him. "What do you think the next year will be like?"

He'd told her earlier that they used to talk about the upcoming year on her birthday. It seemed right to keep with tradition.

"I never know. I've learned it's foolish of me to make plans. God has His own plan for me, and I'm just here to find out what it is."

Camille breathed in and felt his words settle in her middle. She'd been so worked up about her recovery that she hadn't stepped back and thought about the Lord's will for her.

Noah lifted one knee and adjusted himself on the boulder to get comfortable. "What about you?"

"I don't know," she whispered. "I hope it'll be more of this." She gestured between them and leaned in closer. "But hoping for something like that seems too good to be true."

Noah didn't correct her, and her heart sank. She was glad she'd chosen to stay here in Blackwater, but could she keep her relationship with Noah? She knew there was something weighing on him, but she dreaded hearing him say it was her stepdad. She was still so unsure about who to trust and when to dig her boots in and hold her ground. Camille might sleep easier at night if she only knew who to fight for and who to fight against.

"I want more of this," she reiterated.

"Do you know how many times I wanted to jump on a plane to Portland?"

"But you couldn't," she finished, and her heart sank with the realization.

"I couldn't. It was tearing me up inside. It still is in a way. I love you, and I've always loved you. Nothing about that will ever change. But as it stands now, I have some things I have to overcome before we can be out in the open about our relationship. I know we don't parade around town. I don't get to do much outside the firehouse and the ranch, but I *wish* I could tell the world about us. I'm honored to be loved by you. I don't take a second of it for granted."

"But it's something that can be fixed, right?" she asked, daring to hope that a reprieve was coming.

"You'll be the first to know when I figure it out. I need to change some things that are pretty set in stone, and it might not happen fast or at all. There's a lot at stake, but I can't just sit back and not fight for us."

A melancholy cold had fallen over the conversation, and she wanted to change the subject. She scooted closer to him, and he laid back on the rock. Tucking her arms into her chest, she settled in next to him and rested her head on his shoulder. Noah's strong arm wrapped around her, pulling her in closer. She could smell his cologne and turned her face toward him to breathe in deeper.

The night was quiet, and she understood why people sometimes referred to the dark sky as a blanket of stars. She felt wrapped in the comfort of the Wyoming sky. It was thrilling to know that no one else was around for miles. Even though they were on the far side of the ranch, exposed to all the dangers of the night, she felt completely at ease with Noah by her side.

When she spoke, her words were quiet so they wouldn't disrupt the stillness around them. "You ever wonder how long we'll love each other?"

Noah nuzzled into her hair. "I don't plan to ever stop loving you."

"I know, but if we love each other forever, how long is forever? And when will we know when it's the end?"

"I guess we won't, but I really don't care to be around that day. I think I'll call in sick."

Camille chuckled. "You never call in sick." The ranch didn't allow for time off. Not even on rainy days or in the thick of winter. Neither did the fire station.

"I don't," Noah confirmed. "I'm saving it for forever."

CHAPTER 20
NOAH

Stepping into the small local church on Sunday morning was as expected as the sun rising in the east, yet Noah somehow felt different every time. Each week passed much like the one before it, but the wheels of time were turning at an alarming pace these days.

He used to sit on the fifth pew from the front with his family and Camille every time the doors were open. Now, he still sat in the same place, but one person was missing.

It was a blessing that Camille had held onto her faith through everything she'd experienced. A traumatic brain injury could easily change someone's personality entirely. Thankfully, he hadn't seen much of that in Camille. Her memory seemed to be the most affected, but she was still the lively, kind woman he'd known when they were teenagers.

If things settled with Nathan, maybe he could sit beside her through church services again. Where did she attend services these days?

Noah hadn't seen much of Camille since her birthday. He'd worked his 48-hour shift at the fire station, then he'd been needed for a time-sensitive job on the ranch as soon as he pulled up at home. He'd rescheduled his volunteer time at the store this week, and that meant they'd been apart longer than he liked. They'd texted and called regularly, but none of that could compare to seeing her in person.

After working without a break for days on end, Noah craved the rest Camille offered. He wasn't eighteen anymore, and staying up late with Camille on her birthday had started a chain of long nights.

He couldn't really complain, though, because spending time with Camille was worth it. She'd been so happy to sneak out with him and celebrate her birthday, and she'd appreciated his effort to make her day special. Not to mention, she'd also remembered their tradition, which felt like a step in the right direction. He just wished there was more time spent with her and less time spent breaking his back.

Noah took a seat beside Aaron, and then Levi climbed onto the pew beside them. The kid would be squirming and moving from one Harding lap to another until the services began and he was dismissed to the kids' class.

As expected, Levi crawled off to someone else as Aaron turned his attention to Noah. He watched his brother's expression shift to one of concern at something behind him.

Looking over his shoulder, Noah saw Camille standing at the end of the pew. A tan shawl was draped over her shoulders, and her navy dress hung straight to her ankles. She smiled brightly and pulled her Bible closer to her chest.

"Hey."

Her greeting was so bubbly, so why was there a sinking feeling in his gut?

Oh yeah, because they were in a public place, and Aaron was sitting beside him. His brother would no doubt be upset about Camille's sudden appearance. Noah had recently confessed the threat dating Camille put on the ranch and everyone living there. He still didn't have any good or reassuring news for his brother concerning Nathan's threats.

Part of him was jumping for joy at the sight of her, but the other part was curling up in fear. He'd told her they needed to lay low in public, but he hadn't expressed how strict they needed to be or how high the stakes were.

"Hey." Noah stood to pull her into a hug and used the new perspective to take a look around. He couldn't imagine that any of the church regulars even knew about the threat from Nathan, let alone would run off to blab about seeing them together.

Noah knew these people, and he usually felt safe at church from petty things like gossip.

"I wasn't expecting you here this morning." He tried to hide his surprise.

"Well, I wanted to see you, so I figured I might need to find creative ways to spend time with you. I was on my way to church and remembered that you might be going too, so I ended up here." Camille shrugged and smiled.

"And you remembered where I went to church?" he asked.

"I did. I didn't remember the name, but I knew where it was."

Noah motioned for her to sit beside him, and his family scooted down the pew. He tried his best to avoid Aaron's glare, but if looks could kill, Noah would be ashes right now.

The service began, and Noah wrapped Camille's small hand in his as he tried his best to focus on the message. A few times, he'd felt Aaron shift in his seat beside him and found his brother's stare still trained on him. Noah pursed his lips and prayed his brother kept his mouth shut.

Noah knew he was skirting the line with Camille. How far could their relationship go before the reckoning? She'd said she didn't want to know what or who stood between them, but how much longer could they keep going without her knowing?

She would have to know sooner or later. After all, her family was involved.

Her smile and carefree attitude told him she didn't have a clue how big this was, but he didn't want to be the one to burst her bubble. He liked it when she was happy.

And that was all he wanted—for Camille to be happy.

Could he give her that by stepping back and letting her keep the peace in her family?

Noah gritted his teeth through the service and tried not to squeeze Camille's hand too tight. He didn't want her to know about his worries. He'd carry it all if it meant she didn't have to.

When the service was over, Camille greeted his family with a smile. Aaron snaked his way out of the crowd with Levi before Camille even noticed, and Noah watched his cousin, Hunter, trail them to the parking lot.

Outside, Noah walked Camille to her car.

She turned at the driver's side door and smiled. "I'm glad I got to see you. I was afraid you were avoiding me."

He hadn't been avoiding her. It was quite the opposite. He was dying to be with her, but circumstances hadn't allowed it lately.

"I'm definitely not avoiding you. My work schedule gets all clogged up sometimes."

"I understand. I really do. I know you have a lot of responsibilities." Camille reached for his collar and rubbed the material between her fingers. "I just miss you, and I feel like I have a lot of time to make up for."

"I know. I have some work to do at the ranch today, but you're welcome to tag along if you want. It's not the most ideal way to spend time together, but it's something."

"Yes," she agreed. "I'd love to."

"Great."

At least at the ranch, he could spend time with her without worrying about who was watching.

CHAPTER 21

CAMILLE

Noah wasn't kidding when he said sometimes his schedule got hectic. Apparently, summer was hay season, on top of all the other regular duties. After two weeks of scraping for time with him and only seeing him during his volunteer hours at Blackwater Restoration, she decided things had to change. If she wanted to see him, she'd have to go where he went—to the ranch.

Camille sat on the open tailgate as Noah filled the tractors with diesel from the tank truck. She'd started trying to help out while she was there. Some things were easier to understand, while other things were just hard labor. By the end of the second day on the ranch, she knew she needed new shoes and that cowboy hats weren't just a fashion statement.

Despite the heat and the dirt, she treasured the time she spent with Noah there. If she thought she enjoyed watching Noah working at Blackwater Restoration, it was nothing compared to seeing him in his element on the ranch. He made sweaty and dirty look good when he pulled wrenches and threw square bales. He knew what needed to be done, and he did everything effortlessly.

With the patience of a hunter, he answered all of them, sometimes stopping to show her the mechanics of the equipment he was repairing. He even knew what the cows needed just by looking at them. Generational ranchers naturally knew a lot about the animals, since their family passed down information. He could tell her why a cow would pull herself from the herd, and he knew when to supplement or include medication in their feed.

"So how do you keep the animals' water from freezing in the winter?" she asked.

Noah placed the nozzle back in its place and stepped toward her. "We have a trough system that keeps the water moving so we don't have to break the ice every day."

They'd been riding around filling up equipment for a while now, and he always stopped to kiss her on the forehead before getting back in the cab and driving to the next stop.

At the end of a long workday, Noah was covered in dirt and had brown streaks down his face from the sweat tracks. Camille secretly admired him the most then. Most people wouldn't work the land this long for so little pay.

When the sun began to sink, Noah met her at the tailgate and blew out a heavy breath. They still had a little bit of sun left, and she wondered what their next task would be before they ran out of daylight.

"I need a shower, but then I think we need to pick you out a horse." He removed his cowboy hat and rubbed his arm across his forehead. "I have a few hours in the morning before I have to mix some feed. We can take a ride if you're not busy."

Wild horses couldn't keep her away, no matter what she had going on. "Yes! I'd love to." She clapped her hands together excitedly. It'd been years since she'd been on a horse, but she thought she remembered the basics.

"Great." He grinned. "Hop in, and I'll drop you off at the stable, and Lucas can get started with you while I get cleaned up."

He reached across the cab and grabbed her hand as they rode over the soft hills back toward the stables. "Then, I'd like to make you supper."

"Why don't I make supper for you? You've been working all day."

Noah shook his head and smiled. "It'd be foolish of me to turn you down."

He parked the truck just outside the stable and walked inside with her. Lucas was brushing a black mare in the third stall, and he perked up with his usual wide grin when he saw them.

"Hey, Millie!"

"Hey, yourself."

Lucas was probably Noah's friendliest brother. As the youngest, he got away with the most, but thankfully, he didn't abuse his freedom too much. His free spirit made him a perfect companion for horses, and he was their resident expert.

"What brings you to my neck of the woods?"

Noah slung his arm over her shoulder and pulled her in close. "Millie needs a horse. We're ridin' in the morning."

"I gotcha covered." Lucas patted the mare's flank and stepped back. "This here's Sadie, but she's a wild one." He leaned in close to whisper as he passed. "I wouldn't recommend her."

Noah squeezed Camille in close to his chest once more and kissed her forehead. "I'll be right back."

She watched him leave before turning to where Lucas had walked off. She caught up with him at the next stall. "How many horses do you have?"

"Seven. We don't need them every day, but sometimes there are tasks that are easier to do on a horse. If a cow gets off into the woods by herself, sometimes the trees are too close together to take the truck lookin' for her. So we ride. Things like that."

"Gotcha. So, since Sadie is out of the question, who's next?"

Lucas led her to the pasture outside and introduced her to Blane, Vader, Carson, Weston, Sprite, and Skittle. He told her about each horse as if they were people he cared about. He spoke lovingly about them, and she could tell he talked to the horses when he was in the stable alone.

After hearing all about their personalities, quirks, and mannerisms, they decided Sprite was probably the best fit for her, but she wouldn't know for sure until tomorrow when she got a chance to ride her. Another plus was that Sprite got along well with Weston, Noah's horse.

Lucas gave Camille a sugar cube for Sprite, and she giggled as the horse's lips tickled her palm. They led Sprite to the stable and he showed Camille how to groom her and gave her a refresher course on horses. As she stood in the horse's stall getting to know her, Camille asked Lucas the question that had been on her mind for a while.

"What was Noah like while I was gone? I mean, what did I miss?"

"You really want to know?"

When she nodded, he continued.

"He drifted back and forth." Lucas turned his attention to the horse as he stroked Sprite's mane. "Noah has always kept to himself, but sometimes, he was like a lost puppy. Like he didn't know how to do anything but work and sleep. There wasn't much we could do to pull him out of the hole when he dug his boots in. He didn't want to talk about it with anyone."

Camille swallowed hard and sucked in a deep breath before remembering they were in a stable. The smell hit her hard before she stopped the intake, and she covered her nose on instinct.

"Other days, he was mad at the world. We knew to steer clear of him when he got like that. He was like a wolf, ready to fight anyone who dared to look at him the wrong way." Lucas shrugged. "I guess that was the injustice of it all. He never told us why things fell apart when you went to college, but I imagine it wasn't because he wanted it to end."

No, she didn't think it was either, but she couldn't piece together what had actually fallen apart between them—or who was standing in their way.

"That's not the Noah I know," she whispered.

"You're right. It wasn't like him." Lucas turned to her, and his expression was more serious than she'd ever seen. "He isn't himself without you."

The barn door opened, and Lucas called out, "We're in Sprite's stall."

Noah stepped up to the open stall a moment later, looking fresh and ready for the evening ahead. If she hadn't seen it with her own eyes, she'd never guess he'd worked in the field all day.

He leaned against the frame and gave her that grin that lifted one side of his mouth. "You ready?"

"Yep. I think I found my friend," Camille said as she stroked Sprite's neck.

"I thought you'd choose her. She's a good fit for you. Just don't tighten your feet around her sides to slow down like you would a trail riding horse. She's a cutting horse, so that means speed up to her."

"Got it."

They said their good-byes to Lucas, and Camille wondered how much of what Noah's brother had told her had been an exaggeration.

CHAPTER 22
NOAH

Noah followed Camille back to her house without turning the radio on in the truck. The old stereo only worked half the time anyway, and he needed the quiet. If he worked in the fields alone all day, it wasn't uncommon for him to enjoy the silence for the rest of the evening. He used to go days without even speaking to anyone before Camille came along.

But Noah liked talking to her, and it lifted his lonely soul when she asked questions about what he was doing. It wasn't always easy to work with someone new on the ranch. He and his brothers had perfected it over years, but the solution was usually to keep your head down and minimize chitchat.

With Camille, it was different. Explaining a task to her was as easy as breathing. She listened, and he usually had the time to let her give it a try on her own. It was a good thing she wanted to work along-side him. Ranchers didn't have much time during daylight hours to spare for spending time with girl-friends or spouses, but he knew Camille wouldn't let that stop her. Knowing she loved the ranch as much as he did eased some of his worries, but would she eventually grow tired of the lifestyle?

Noah pulled into Camille's drive and parked behind her 4Runner. She jumped out and waited for him to catch up to her before grabbing his hand to walk inside together.

She closed the door of her house and locked them away from the rest of the world for a little while. What would it be like to come home to Camille every evening? Would they live in his old cabin? She might not be comfortable there.

He scanned the living area, taking in the layout and design. "You have a nice place."

Camille shrugged. "I like it. I'm not here a lot, so I don't need much."

To his surprise, the space was minimal, but he could pick out some of her touches—a small owl figurine made of scrap metal on the hearth, a rough wooden breakfast table, a bookend in the shape of a squirrel. Camille had always been one for the small woodland creatures.

Noah could imagine she had the money to live wherever she wanted in Blackwater or even Cody. She'd mentioned working for a corporate firm since graduation, and he would bet she'd kept a steady job through undergrad and law school.

Noah followed her into the kitchen and watched as she opened and closed cabinets.

"I can make fried pork chops or..."

When she trailed off in thought, Noah answered. "Pork chops sound great."

Camille opened the fridge. "All right. You want something to drink?"

He accepted a glass of water and stood near the sink, while she gathered the ingredients she'd need from the four corners of the kitchen.

"How can I help?"

Camille shook her head. "You can't. I'm making supper. Sit down and take a load off. Go watch TV or something." She shooed him out of the kitchen.

He spotted a recliner in the living room where he could lean back and still watch her in the kitchen. Folding his arms across his chest, he settled in. Her long black ponytail swished with every change in direction the way it did when they danced that one night. She knew her way around a kitchen the way he knew the ranch.

The next thing he knew, someone was tapping his shoulder.

"Noah, supper is ready. Are you hungry?"

His eyes opened lazily, and he cleared his throat. Camille stood over him with a questioning look on her face.

"If you want to keep sleeping, I can reheat the food later."

Noah sat up. "I can't believe I fell asleep."

Camille chuckled low. "I can. You worked like a mule today."

Rubbing the sleep from his eyes, he stood and stretched his back. "It smells delicious."

Three quick knocks came from the front door, and they both turned as if they'd see the visitor through the solid wood. When silence followed, they looked at each other.

Camille shook her head. "I'm not expecting anyone."

Noah shrugged, and she moved to answer it.

"There you are!" Camille's mother, Bonnie, said as she stepped inside and wrapped one arm around her daughter. "I've been calling you."

Camille hugged her mother with one arm and stuttered, "Um, I didn't pay much attention to my phone today. I'm sorry."

"You had me worried."

Noah stood paralyzed. Bonnie would tell Nathan she saw Noah at Camille's house, and whatever retribution her stepdad had planned would come crashing down on the Hardings.

Bonnie turned his way and raised her hand to her mouth. "I'm sorry." Her smile grew wider, but it wasn't malicious. "I didn't know you had company."

Camille looked at him, and the worry on her face

told him she already had an idea about what—or who—was intent on keeping them apart. "Yeah, Noah volunteers at Blackwater Restoration."

She didn't mention their relationship, and he wanted to sigh in relief and crawl into a hole at the same time. This was her family they were hiding from, and it wasn't as if she were a rebellious teenager. Camille was an adult, and Noah was a decent man with a steady job, if her stepdad allowed him to keep it.

"Oh." Bonnie's eyebrows rose in appreciation. "I didn't know that. You were always so generous with your time, Noah, especially when it came to things that were important to our Millie."

"Actually, Mom, he was volunteering there before I got the job."

Camille was doing everything she could to steer her mother away from suspicions about the seriousness of their connection. Camille was a smart woman, and it seemed she'd caught on, whether she wanted to or not.

Bonnie reached out her arms to him. "You're such a good man, Noah. I missed you when Millie moved off."

Noah returned Bonnie's hug and gave Camille a panicked look over her mother's shoulder. Bonnie had always liked him, and he truly believed she didn't even know about Nathan's threats. Her heart was as pure as Camille's.

"I missed both of you," Noah said.

Bonnie pulled back and looked him up and down. "I don't think I got to properly thank you for what you did for Camille. You saved her life! I just got so caught up in caring for her that I forgot to reach out."

Noah held up a hand. "I was happy to do it. I'm glad she's safe."

Bonnie turned quickly between the two of them. "Oh! This must mean she remembers you!"

Camille rubbed her arms for comfort. "Some. Noah has been great about helping me fill in the blanks."

Bonnie clasped her hands to her chest. "I've been praying Camille would find something—or someone—who could help with her recovery. It's been so hard on her."

Noah peeked at Camille and saw her gaze move to the floor as she bit the corner of her mouth.

"I think she's doing an amazing job on her own," Noah said. "Injuries like this take a lot of time and patience."

Bonnie patted his shoulder. "You're sweet to help her." Her eyes grew wide in realization. "Oh, goodness. Am I interrupting?"

Camille pointed toward the kitchen. "We were about to have supper. You want to join us?"

"No, no. I just dropped by to check on you since I

couldn't get you on the phone. I have to get home. Nathan will be expecting me."

The mention of their thief of joy sent a chill down Noah's spine. He hoped Camille knew of a way to prevent her mother from sharing the news about his presence here tonight with Nathan.

"Right. Well, thanks for coming to check on me, and again, I'm sorry I didn't keep my phone closer." Camille leaned in to hug her mother again.

"It's okay, sweetie. I just worry about you all the time since the accident." Bonnie leaned back and brushed the flyaways from Camille's face. "I love you more than you know."

"I love you too, Mom."

Bonnie turned to Noah and waved. "It was so good to see you. I hope we'll be seeing more of you."

"You too, Mrs. Vanderbilt."

She flicked her wrist at him as she walked out the door. "Oh, it's Bonnie. You're such a gentleman."

Camille closed the door behind her mother and turned to Noah. Their previous happy mood was over, and he wasn't sure he could eat anything now. His stomach churned as his worries escalated. Any time he'd thought he had to make things right was gone.

CHAPTER 23
NOAH

Noah nudged his horse, Weston, closer to Camille's blue roan, Sprite. They'd been riding since just before sunrise, and they hadn't spoken much. Actually, they'd both remained fairly quiet since Camille's mother had stopped by the night before. Noah certainly didn't know what to say, and Camille seemed at a loss for words too.

The silence wasn't tense, but there were things not being said. Instead, they'd kept their conversation generic. She pointed out a patch of wildflowers and several hawks circling overhead between the stretches of horse hooves clopping on the dry dirt.

When Noah's horse fell into step beside Sprite, Camille's smile told him she was strong enough to handle what was coming.

"I'll figure this out. Don't worry." He reached out a hand, and she placed hers in his with a smile.

"I know I told you I didn't want to know what was going on, but I think I figured it out anyway." She turned her gaze from him to look at the open pasture ahead of them. "This could be bigger than I thought."

Noah didn't confirm her suspicion.

Camille turned back to him, her brow slightly furrowed. "I want you to know that we're in this together." She gave his hand a slight squeeze before releasing it. "You can talk about it with me, and if there's anything I can do to help, let me. You don't have to do it alone. I know it's weighing on you."

Noah shook his head. "I'm pretty sure you know who it is. I don't know if it's something you can fix."

"I still feel like I don't know him that well. I know Nathan cares about me, but only if he can control what I do. Maybe it wasn't that way before, but it sure seems like I took a lot of his advice."

"He's been there for you and your mom for years. He adopted you when you were still young. I knew this would be hard for you, and that's why I've been afraid to bring it up. You shouldn't have to choose between me and your family. I want you to have it all. I'm willing to get along with him, but I'm not anywhere near the social standing Nathan Vanderbilt will allow for his only daughter."

Camille trained her gaze on the worn path ahead of them. "Let me think about how to broach the subject with him. Maybe I can talk to Mom."

"I plan to talk to Nathan. I've been thinking and praying about what to say to him, but seeing your mom last night has kind of moved up any timeline I might have set for myself. He'll know about us soon, if not already."

"I don't know how intent he is on making sure you and I stay away from each other, but I know he has money and influence. Would he really do something dangerous?" Camille questioned.

Noah shrugged. "The threats he made before you left for college were pretty clear. After your wreck, he told me at the hospital that his demands still stand."

Camille shook her head and huffed. Her nostrils flared with injustice. "How could he do this? What does it matter to him who I love?"

"It's always been about appearances with Nathan. He pulls the strings in this area of Wyoming, and he always gets his way. To him, showing that his family is poised and perfect is a sign of strength." Noah turned to watch her reaction to his next words. "His only daughter marrying a rancher isn't ideal when she could marry a lawyer or a politician."

Camille's nose scrunched up in distaste. "Who cares if he wants me to marry a socialite? I plan on marrying a rancher, and I'd like to see him stop me."

Noah's breath caught in his lungs. She would marry him? He'd always hoped she would, but there had always been a nagging voice in the back of his head that said she might think of him as a fling, rather than someone to settle down and grow old with.

Camille smiled wide at what could only be a gaping expression on his face. "Keep praying about it. We just need some guidance."

Noah barely registered her words before she was tightening her feet and grabbing onto the reins. Sprite shot off down the lane ahead of him, and Noah spurred Weston into action.

Camille's hair flew behind her in the wind as she leaned over Sprite's mane. She might as well be a hawk flying in the wide-open Wyoming sky. The horse was her wings, and she was meant for a life here where she could embrace the land and the animals she loved.

Noah galloped up beside her, and the twinkle in her dark-brown eyes had him smiling so hard that his cheeks ached.

How had Camille ended up in a family who valued money over happiness? When did material things become more important than loving the people who filled our hearts with joy?

That wasn't Camille. God had a plan for her, and Noah had to believe that she would end up settling in this place. A place they both loved.

Camille left around noon, and Noah still had work to do. He'd promised to check the fences and decided to just stay on his horse when telling her good-bye. After riding the perimeter, he put Weston in the horse pasture and drove the fuel truck into town to fill up. He stopped at the hardware store and picked up the list of things Micah had given him, paid the Lawrences a visit for some eggs, and loaded up at the feed and seed.

He made it back to the ranch for supper and ignored glances from Hunter and Aaron throughout the meal. Aaron must have told their cousin about the threat hanging over them.

Hunter wasn't one to mess with, and he had just as much loyalty to the ranch as the brothers did, if not more, but the supper table wasn't the place to voice their opinions about Camille. Mama didn't put up with raised voices in her vicinity.

When everyone had finished eating, Noah volunteered to help clean up. With the main room and kitchen cleaned up, he propped against a counter in the industrial-size kitchen.

When his brothers had left and only his parents remained, Noah said, "I need to talk to both of you about something."

His dad gave him his attention, but his mother stepped closer to whisper, "Are you gonna ask her to marry you?"

Her voice was so full of excitement, and he hated to burst her bubble. "Not exactly."

How could he explain this to his parents? He mumbled to himself, "Where to start?"

With a heavy sigh he began. "I'm not supposed to be in a relationship with Camille. Nathan Vanderbilt laid down the law when I snuck her off to Colorado after we graduated."

"Oh, I remember that," Silas Harding recalled.

"Yeah, not my brightest moment," Noah admitted as his knuckles turned white gripping the edge of the counter. "Anyway, he told me back then, if I didn't let her go off to college and cut all ties, he'd make sure the whole ranch would crumble."

His mother raised a hand to her mouth and clutched a dish rag in the other. "Oh, Noah."

He swallowed hard and cleared his throat. "He said she was a Vanderbilt, and he wouldn't stand for her running around with a Harding anymore." Noah raised his head and met his father's stare. "I'm not the man he wants her to end up with."

"But that was years ago," his mother pointed out.

Noah shook his head. "He reminded me of his threat at the hospital after she had her wreck."

His mother's mouth pursed as she tried to contain her mounting frustration.

"I know he's capable of it," Noah admitted. "He's

closed half a dozen businesses in town, and shuttin' down a ranch would be nothing to him."

His dad still hadn't said a word. Noah was sure the old man was waiting for Noah to say his piece.

"I don't want to lose her again." Noah's voice broke on the last word. "I don't want to lose her again, but I can't change who I am. It isn't my personality he doesn't like. He won't stand for a rancher as his son-in-law." Noah threw his hands out to his sides.

Silas stepped closer to Noah. "I see the problem." He bowed his head and shook it slowly, thinking. "I wish I had the answers for you, but I know nothing, and I act like I know less than that."

That wasn't true. His dad was the wisest person Noah knew, but Silas had changed since his heart attack. He was calmer and more easygoing. But right now, Noah needed the stern man he'd looked up to while growing up.

"But I know one thing," his dad continued. "This isn't your fault or Camille's. Nathan Vanderbilt has made some decisions out of hatred and fear of the things he doesn't understand. There's only so much you can do to reach him, but after that, leave the rest to the Lord. You manage your life, and we'll manage the ranch. We need to have faith that God will change Nathan's heart."

That wasn't necessarily a solution, like Silas had said, but it was a start in the right direction. Noah knew he had to talk to Nathan, but what he was meant to say when he got there was another story.

"I'm proud of you, son." Silas laid his hand on Noah's shoulder. "You shouldn't have to live your life under someone else's thumb. Your mom and I will be praying things can work out between the two of you before innocent people are put out of a job and a home."

His dad looked to his mom, and she slid in next to his side. Silas wrapped his arm around his wife and continued, "Until then, we'll prepare ourselves in the event that he carries out his threats."

When Noah had come to his parents, he hadn't known what they would say. They could've easily told him to cut Camille out of his life to save their family the way he'd done all those years ago.

Instead, they'd rallied behind him, ready to support his decision to build a life with the woman he loved. He imagined his father wouldn't have taken the same threats as lightly if they'd been against him and his mother when they were young.

His mom wrapped him in a hug with tears in her eyes.

"It's okay, Mom. I'm gonna try my best to fix it. I won't let him take the ranch."

His mom whispered broken words in his ear, "It's gonna be okay."

CHAPTER 24
CAMILLE

Camille was awake, dressed, and pulling up at Blackwater Ranch before sunrise. Noah said that he and a ranch hand named Jameson were taking some calves to the auction today, and she'd asked if she could tag along. Granted, all of that had been before she knew she needed to get up before the roosters.

She parked next to the main house and grabbed her new cowboy hat out of the passenger seat. She'd gotten a walnut colored one to match Noah's, and she was beginning to feel lost without it.

She spotted Noah by the truck with the trailer behind it and waved. Trotting up beside him, she wrapped her arms around his neck and gave him a quick kiss. "Morning, handsome."

"Morning, beautiful."

Camille looked around and realized the calves were already loaded. "How long have you been up?"

"I've been out and about since five. We separated the calves yesterday, but I still needed to load them when the sun came up."

And she'd been silently groaning about their six a.m. meeting. "Do you sleep?"

Noah rubbed the back of his neck. "On occasion."

A tall man with broad shoulders and a jaw full of whiskers stepped around the truck and noticed her. He lifted his hand and greeted her warmly. "Hey, there. I'm Jameson. You must be Camille. Everyone around here's been talking about you." He gripped her hand and shook gently. "I didn't know what to expect because some of the Hardings think you hung the moon and some of 'em kinda don't think you should be hanging around at all."

"I think that's enough, Jameson," Noah said in a stern voice. "Jameson works part-time on the ranch, and we're in the same crew at the fire station."

"Yeah, I was there when you had that wreck last year."

"Really?" Camille was suddenly interested in Jameson.

"Yeah, that was a bad one." Jameson shook his head. "Noah was a basket case, and I just didn't know what to say to calm him down."

Camille could guess there wasn't anything he could've said to calm Noah down. She hated thinking about what it must have been like for Noah to see her like that. The morning was warm, but Camille wrapped her arms around her middle for comfort.

"I'm glad you were there. Thanks for anything you did to help."

Jameson tilted his hat toward her. "Nothin' to it. I'm glad you're doing okay."

All three of them climbed into the truck and headed down the road. Camille filled Jameson in on some stories from Noah's teen years that she'd remembered. Noah smiled and let her laugh with Jameson about the things they'd done and the trouble they'd gotten into in their younger years. Then she quizzed both of the men about the auction. She hadn't been to a cattle auction before, and she was excited to see what it looked like.

When they arrived, it ended up being about what she expected from Noah and Jameson's explanations. Cows in herds or individually were wrangled into a pen and showcased, while buyers examined them and did their bidding. There was a lot of waiting around, but everyone seemed to be talking and catching up.

Noah said the auctions happened every weekend, but their ranch didn't always have cattle to auction. Right now, they were separating the nursing cows from the calves so the ranch could get the milk.

When they'd sold all the cattle they came with, Noah held her back before she could jump into the truck. "Can we ditch him somewhere close by?"

Camille chuckled low and swatted his chest. Jameson had been a fun companion today, laughing and joking with them, and he'd even taken over most of the auction duties so that she and Noah could spend time together.

She leaned in close to whisper in his ear. "When we get back, drop him off, and I'll cook you a steak tonight."

Noah's eyes drifted closed as he whispered back, "I love it when you talk pretty to me."

He was close enough that his warm breath tickled her cheek. She turned a fraction of an inch, and Noah sealed their lips in a heart-stopping kiss. His strong arms wrapped around her waist, and she latched onto his shoulders.

This was the man she wanted to spend the rest of her life with. There was a rancher who lived in a tiny cabin who owned her heart. Where he lived or the work he did had never mattered when it came to her love for him.

Her heart was as wide open as the plains and as full and tall as the Rockies. Home would always be wherever Noah was, and that meant her home was Blackwater Ranch.

C amille fell into bed at eleven that night. Noah had come over for supper, and they'd sat on the couch talking while reruns of *Friends* played on the TV. It'd been a long day at the auction, and the heat had drained all her energy.

Remembering that she'd left her cell in the kitchen, she grunted and threw the covers off to retrieve it. She forgot about her phone a lot these days, and that meant missing calls from her mom more often than she liked.

She had two missed calls from her mom and one from Jenny. It was too late to call Mom back, so she crawled back into bed and sent a quick text apologizing for missing her calls before pressing the button to dial Jenny's number.

"Hello."

"Hey, is it too late to call?" Camille asked.

"No, I was just catching up on my devotionals. How was your day?"

Camille and Jenny usually talked once in the mornings and once in the evenings. After being roommates through college, it'd been hard for the cousins to separate when Jenny moved back to Wyoming. After the wreck, Jenny became Camille's lifeline, helping her navigate a world she didn't understand anymore.

Now, Camille knew that Jenny had been giving

Noah updates about her from the beginning. He'd shared that with Camille after her birthday. It had endeared him to her even more knowing that Noah had been concerned about her after he'd been shut out by her family.

"It was good. I went with Noah to a cattle auction, and he came over for supper."

"Are things getting serious?"

Camille tugged on the end of a strand of her long dark hair. "I don't know. The short answer is yes, but the real answer is I don't know if Nathan is okay with any of this."

"I really don't have any advice for you. I wish I knew what to tell you."

"I know now that Nathan doesn't want us together, but Noah seems really worked up about it. I just don't know how serious this threat is." Camille paused to choose her words carefully. "Is Nathan dangerous?"

Jenny huffed a sigh. "I'd like to say no. Nathan has been in our family for over a decade, and he's always been good to us. He took you in as his own, and he was always kind to me."

"What's the but?"

"But everyone in town knows he's ruthless in business."

"But this isn't business. This is my life," Camille reminded Jenny.

"I know. Trust me, I know. I don't want to

believe it, but the truth is Nathan kept Noah from seeing you at the hospital after your wreck. It makes me think he really could be the reason Noah cut ties with you after you left for college."

"Oh, I'm pretty sure he's the reason. You should've seen Noah's face when Mom showed up that time when he was here. He looked like he'd been shot."

"Then I think we have our answer. Whatever Nathan said to Noah, it must have been serious. I doubt it was anything that would harm another person, but Nathan has pull around here that we can't even understand."

"What could he possibly do that would have Noah scared like that if it wasn't harming someone?"

Jenny yawned. "I'm not sure, but I don't want to find out. Have you talked to him?"

"Nathan?" Camille asked.

"Yeah."

"Actually, I haven't talked to him much at all since the wreck. I didn't remember him at first, and I think it hurt his feelings. He doesn't call me a lot, but he's nice to me when I have meals with him and Mom."

"That sounds about right."

"But he hasn't said a word about Noah, and neither have I. I'm scared to think the idea in my head is the reason he is shaken up about moving our relationship forward. I know he wants to be with me, but there are times when I feel him pulling away." Camille turned off the lamp on her nightstand. "I feel like I'm running in circles thinking about it. Maybe it'll just take time for me to get comfortable with Nathan again."

"It'll come. I'm praying for you. Love you."

"Love you too. Thanks for always being there for me."

"You'd do the same for me. Good night."

Camille rolled over in bed thinking about the people in her life that were constant. Her mom would always be there for her—Jenny too. Nathan seemed like a constant, but for some reason, she felt like she knew the least about him.

And then there was Noah. He was important to her, and that meant something when uncertainty followed her everywhere. If her heart and her head were in agreement, she should listen to them.

Noah had been by her side almost as long as her family, and she knew not to let someone go if they chose to carve out a part of their life for her.

Camille prayed for guidance and understanding. Then she fell into a peaceful sleep thinking about Bluestone Creek and the brown-eyed man who held her heart.

CHAPTER 25
NOAH

Camille's parents' house was a log and brick monstrosity with wooden columns along the front side thicker than Noah had ever seen. Two stories of walls and windows stretched into a double-decker garage on one side. A twenty-foot-tall statue of angels and cherubs sat imposing in the grassy area along the circular drive.

He'd put off coming here for long enough, but it was time to talk. If Nathan wasn't home, he'd just sit in his truck and wait for him.

Noah had always felt small when he came here. The size of the place dwarfed anything around it except the mountains. He knew from days past when he would visit Camille that there was a heated pool in the back along with a fire pit, an outdoor grilling area, and a guest house.

The old truck door groaned and creaked as it

closed behind him, and Noah threw his cowboy hat back into the cab through the open window. There wasn't any sense in stirring the pot. His boots thudded loudly against the sturdy boards of the porch as he approached the door. A video doorbell that had no doubt already announced his presence hung on the wall beside the entrance.

He knew what he needed to do today. He needed to convince the man who hated him that he was really a good guy. He needed to make the wealthiest man in Blackwater see that living on the ranch wasn't so bad, and that it was what Camille wanted. He needed to tell Nathan all of those things and make him understand how much he loved Camille.

He touched the button, and the door opened within seconds.

Nathan answered with his chin lifted.

Noah shifted his weight to his other foot. "Mr. Vanderbilt, can I have a moment of your time?"

Nathan looked much the same as he had before Camille left for college. His salt-and-pepper hair gave him a distinguished look, but his eyes dared Noah to tread lightly.

Before Nathan could respond, Bonnie stepped up behind her husband.

"Noah, I was wondering when we would be seeing you." Her usually peppy demeanor was in full swing. "Come on in."

Nathan stepped aside, and Noah cautiously

moved into the entryway. The Vanderbilt home was just as cavernous as he remembered. Every inch of the place screamed opulence. The skylights, the vaulted ceilings, the enormous chandeliers—everything was over the top. It couldn't have been more different from the home Camille was renting in town.

Bonnie ushered Noah into the sitting area, and he took a seat on a fluffy loveseat.

"Can I get you something to drink?"

"I'm fine," Noah replied. It was nice to know that his battle wasn't against both of Camille's parents, but it didn't make what he came here to do any easier.

Nathan touched Bonnie's arm as she walked by him. "I think we need a moment alone."

Bonnie glanced from her husband to Noah and grinned. From the look on her face, Noah imagined she probably thought he was here to ask Nathan's blessing to marry their daughter.

In a way, he was here for that very reason. He wanted to marry Camille more than anything, but gaining Nathan's blessing seemed like a lost cause right about now.

"Sure," Bonnie said. "I'll just be in the kitchen if you need me."

Bonnie hadn't been born into money, and she'd been an average middle-class American until she married Nathan. Noah hadn't known Camille's dad, but he didn't doubt that Camille got her kind heart from her mother.

When Bonnie was out of sight, Nathan leaned back in his chair, relaxing. "What brings you here?"

Noah sat up straighter and faced Nathan. "I just want to talk. I know you said your thoughts on Camille and I dating hadn't changed when she was in the hospital, but I want you to know that I can't leave her alone. I need her in my life, and I love her—"

Nathan interrupted. "You're right. Things haven't changed. I suggest you stop pouring out your heart now."

An ache began to grow in Noah's chest. "Please, Mr. Vanderbilt. I just think you should know that she means the world to me. I'll do everything in my power to give her the best, and—"

"And what? You can't afford the best of anything. She deserves more than an old shack on a farm." Nathan scooted to the edge of his seat and leaned forward. "I adopted Camille into the Vanderbilt family when she was eleven. She is *my* daughter now, and I won't let her waste her life in the backwoods of some cattle farm."

"She loves the ranch—"

"That's ridiculous!" he shouted. "Camille should be studying for the Bar exam, not hanging out in a stable."

Nathan stood as if the conversation were over.

It couldn't be over; Noah hadn't convinced him that he'd be a good husband for Camille. What else could he say?

Noah stood to keep the playing field even. "Mr. Vanderbilt, I love her. I can't just let her go." Noah's arms spread open as wide as his heart.

Nathan moved closer to Noah, and the old man's voice grew deep and low. "You *will* let her go. I heard you were at her house the other night. That won't happen again. I don't want her at the ranch again. I thought I made myself clear when you were eighteen, but I guess you didn't understand." Nathan pointed at Noah. "You don't get to make the rules here. I'm the one who will make sure your family loses every acre of that ranch if I catch you with her again. Do I make myself clear?"

Panic rose in Noah's throat. "You can't. You would take their jobs and their homes just to make sure we're not together? Why?"

"Because you're not good enough for a Vanderbilt!" Nathan's volume rose. "You're a dirty cowboy. I won't allow my daughter to sink so low."

"Mr. Vanderbilt, what can I do to change your mind?" Noah was pleading, desperate and scared. He had no pull in this situation, and all the love he had for Camille couldn't change Nathan's mind.

"You can't." Nathan's gaze traveled down Noah's plaid shirt and faded jeans and back up again. "You can't change who you are." Nathan gestured toward the front door. "I think we're done here."

"Wait, you don't understand—"

"I do understand. And you need to learn when the negotiations are over."

Wrath consumed Noah, and his nostrils flared. "You can't do this."

"Oh, I can." Nathan's evil chuckle echoed in the room. "Keep it up, boy, and I'll make sure there isn't an acre in Wyoming owned by a Harding. I'll take everything from you."

Noah took two deep breaths, chest rising and falling, before he stormed past Nathan and out the door. When he reached his truck, he slid in and slammed the door. His pulse pounded in his ears as he tried to calm his racing heart in the quiet truck. How had that meeting gone so wrong? It hadn't even gotten off the ground before he'd been shut down.

Starting the truck, he prayed. But his desperate prayer was drowned out by Nathan's threats.

I'll take everything from you.

Noah couldn't understand how Nathan could be so closed to the idea that Camille could be happy with him. She would be, wouldn't she?

What did he really have to offer her? A tiny cabin on a wide-open piece of land, a life of hard work, midnight calls to help birth a calf?

Not a bit of that sounded like something Camille

would really want. It was all fun and games right now because it wasn't her way of life—the work that put food on her family's table.

Noah shifted the truck into gear and knew what he had to do. His heart ached with every mile he drove toward Camille's house.

CHAPTER 26

CAMILLE

Camille leaned closer to the screen of her laptop and squinted. "Those might work," she mumbled to herself. The boots on her screen resembled the ones Noah and his brothers wore around the ranch, but finding the female equivalent had proven to be a challenge. Plus, ordering shoes online was always hit or miss. She ran the heart pendant of her necklace back and forth along the chain as she added the boots to the shopping cart.

She'd wised up with the wide-brimmed cowboy hat already, and good boots were a must at this point if she planned to keep working with Noah around the ranch on her days off.

A knock sounded at her door, and Camille jumped in her seat, bumping her knees on the desk. "Oww." So much for assessing the stranger at her door before revealing she was at home.

She pushed away from the desk and padded over to the door in her bare feet. Peering through the peephole, she saw Noah standing on her doorstep with his hands in the front pockets of his jeans.

Camille fumbled with the lock and opened the door, eager to let him in. She didn't really care if he saw her in her red flannel sweatpants and *Ghostbusters* T-shirt.

"Hey!" She grabbed his hand and tugged him inside before closing the door behind him and wrapping him in a hug. He smelled good, and she nuzzled into his chest as his arms settled around her. She closed her eyes to savor the moment.

She lifted her head and rose onto her toes to plant a sweet, slow kiss on his lips. Noah pulled her closer and a groan sounded in his throat. She wrapped her arms around his neck, but he pulled back and released her suddenly.

Trying not to read too much into the distance he'd placed between them, she picked up his hand and pulled him back with her to the desk. "What brings you here tonight? I was just ordering some boots online, and I need your help."

When he didn't respond, she turned back to him and realized his face was pale. "Are you okay? You don't look so good."

Noah swallowed hard and his shoulders drooped. His gaze was focused on her computer. "Boots are really something you should buy in a store. You'll need to try them on, and it'll take a while to break them in."

She shrugged and sat down in front of the laptop. "I figure that won't take long if you keep working me two days a week." She winked at him before scrolling down the page. "I was actually ordering test prep books for the Wyoming Bar exam, but I got tired of that. I was thinking about you and thought I needed some good working boots to wear at the ranch."

"You want to practice law again?" he asked.

Camille shrugged. "I think I might. I would open my own practice this time, and I really want to focus on family law—adoptions and guardianship mostly." Changing the subject quickly, she pointed at the computer screen. "What about these?"

When Noah didn't respond, she looked over her shoulder to find him propped against the back of the couch looking at the floor.

"Noah, what's wrong? You haven't said much tonight." She stood from her chair and went to him, but he didn't look up at her. "Noah?"

His chin lifted at his name, and his breathing was labored.

She rubbed her hand over the stubble on his cheek and tilted her head. "What's wrong?"

He chewed his lip before answering her. "This isn't going to work."

"*What* isn't going to work?"

Noah rubbed a hand over his head and sighed. "Us. We're just too different. You don't really want to haul hay and herd cattle around. You want to be a lawyer, and you should be. That's who you are."

"Wait. What?" Camille lifted her hand between them. "Excuse me, but you don't sound like yourself. Are you trying to break up with me? Because that's not happening. Both of us know we're perfect for each other." She let her hands fall to her sides and focused on breathing evenly. "What's with the sudden doom and gloom?"

"Did you really think it would work?" Noah asked. "You think you'd be happy living in that old cabin with me on a dusty ranch all by ourselves? You'd get tired of that in a hurry. Everyone does. That cabin doesn't even have a TV or internet. You couldn't work from home."

"So?" Camille interrupted. Her volume was rising with his, and she could feel her cheeks heating.

Noah sat up taller and leveled his stare at her. "You think a life working the land, mixing feed, fixing balers, and gettin' up before dawn to do it is the life? Well, it's not!"

Camille clenched her jaw and held her breath. He wasn't doing this to them. Not again.

Noah stood up, forcing Camille to back away. He paced the small area in front of her desk, deciding his next words. "That's the life of a rancher's wife,

Camille. It's not pretty. Would you send me off to work two days at the fire station and then fight for anything that was left of me after the ranch got the majority of the other days?" He jabbed a finger into his chest and gritted his teeth. "That's what you're in for, and I can't let you do it."

She stared him down, holding her ground. "You don't get to decide for me, Noah."

He'd just tried to scare her off with talk of a rancher's wife, but Camille Vanderbilt wasn't one to be shoved around. Not anymore. Nathan had done that, and she'd ended up at a job she hated in a place that wasn't home. She wouldn't let that happen again. She was making her own decisions now.

"You'd stick around because of your loyalty, but you'd be unhappy. I can't let that happen to you. To us."

"That's an excuse," Camille fumed. "I know things won't be easy, but I'm happy as long as I'm with you!"

Noah swallowed hard. "I can't do this."

"Oh, but you will, Noah Harding. I don't run scared, and I won't let you do it either."

Noah tucked his chin and shook his head. "It won't work, Millie. Just let it go."

He was the root of all of her memories. He'd helped her remember a boy who hadn't given up on her when she was young and afraid to lose him if they crossed the line of friendship into something more. He'd given her new memories and filled her days with happiness and hope. He pushed her to find the good in every day and hold onto it because sometimes, memories of the good are what get you through the bad.

Oh, and she knew the bad *would* come. It was knocking on her door right now, begging to be let in.

Camille tried to hide the tremble in her voice, but the traitorous shake made its way out anyway. "Don't do this."

She swallowed hard and blinked to keep the tears from escaping. Camille wasn't a crier, and she wasn't about to start now.

"I have to." He raised his head to look at her and murmured, "I have to go."

"Don't go," she pleaded, trying to stop him from walking away.

"I'll see you around. We just... It wouldn't have worked out for us."

"Stop saying that!" Panic rose in her throat, and she was grasping at anything to keep him there. "You don't mean it."

Noah's gaze traveled to the door, and he tried to step around her.

"Oh, no you don't." She laid her hand on his chest, stopping him. "We are *not* finished."

Noah looked like he was going to be sick. "I have to go."

"You're not running from me again!"

Noah said the words as if he were reading from a script. "I have to go."

Frustration washed over her, and she let her hand drop from his chest. Noah didn't move at first, but after a few seconds, he walked to the door and shut it behind him without looking back.

Her chest was hollow. She felt empty inside, and she hugged her middle as if she could stop herself from breaking apart.

Noah should be here. He was the one who could hold her pieces together. Who would remind her of who she really was now? Who would encourage her and lift her up? Those were the things Noah did every day without thinking twice, just because of who he was and the kind of relationship they had.

Her traitorous tears spilled out along with a sob. This wasn't just about her. Who would remind Noah that he was enough—more than enough? He was all she'd ever wanted. Who would keep him smiling after long days on the farm or responding to calls where he saw terrible things that she couldn't even imagine? Remembering what Lucas had told her in the stable, she knew this wasn't what Noah really wanted.

She clutched the necklace he'd given her a month ago. He was good at so many things—taking care of people, watching over the livestock, providing for his family—but of all the things he did well, he was the best at loving her.

So what if he was gone two days out of every week? She might not see him as much as she wanted, but she wouldn't be lonely. She'd tag along and help him as much as she could on her days off like she'd been doing. Plus, there were too many Hardings at Blackwater Ranch to ever be truly lonely.

But Noah had just ripped that away from her too —that family that she thought of as her own when no one was around to tell her it wasn't the truth.

Confusion and fear swirled in her heart as she sank to the floor and cried all the tears she'd been holding in her entire life. Noah loved her, and she couldn't understand why he would run.

She sucked in a breath and covered her mouth at the realization. What if it was Nathan? Had something happened today? It was after ten o'clock at night, and she wanted to call her mom. Would her mom even know if Nathan was plotting to keep her and Noah apart?

It seemed silly when she thought about it that way. Her stepdad had better things to do than meddle in her love life, but why else would Noah break things off with her so suddenly? There had to be someone pulling strings.

She wanted to believe that Noah still loved her. Whatever doubts he was having, they didn't add up when she remembered the way he'd told her he loved her just this morning. She'd give him a couple of days and call him to talk it out. His shift at the fire station started early in the morning, and he needed to be focused to do his job. But after that, she was going to get the truth out of Noah, whether he liked it or not.

CHAPTER 27
NOAH

Noah closed Camille's door behind him, but it didn't block out her sobs. He couldn't move his feet to walk away from her just yet. What had he done? He'd made things worse with Nathan tonight, and then... this.

Remembering the look on Camille's face had his gut twisting. The last thing he wanted to do was hurt her. He'd been given the chance to be happy again, and it had all been taken away too soon.

Anger built in his chest as he sat on the small step on her front porch. There was a roaring in his ears, but he could still hear Camille's wails behind him.

He wanted to go back inside and hold her and tell her they would make it through anything together.

But he couldn't do that when it was probably a

lie. How could he save his family and keep Camille in his life? It was too much to hope. He'd been allowed to enjoy the best times of his life with her, and the stretches of time in between were just filler.

Sitting alone in the dark night outside her door, he hung his head and prayed.

Lord, where did I go wrong? Why couldn't I fix this? I thought she would be my future, but it feels like You're telling me we're not meant to be.

He scrubbed his hands over his face and sighed.

She was good for me, Lord. She's so good. He swallowed a lump in his throat and rubbed at his tingling eyes. *I don't think I can fix this on my own. I need your help, but I feel lost.*

Lost. He was lost without her, and the Lord wasn't sending him any clear sign.

When the muffled sounds inside Camille's house had silenced, he stood and made his way to his beat-up truck. Just another reminder—staring him in the face—that he wasn't good enough for her.

The rumbling of the truck engine wasn't enough to drown out his spiraling thoughts. This was one of those rare times when he wished the radio worked. The longer he sat in silence, the hotter the fire stoked within him. His helplessness was morphing into fear and anger.

Noah drove too fast along the dirt path leading to his cabin and slammed on the brakes at the last minute, barely stopping at the edge of the porch. A shadow on the small front porch of his house moved as he threw the truck into park and killed the engine.

Hunter stood from the wooden rocking chair. Three steps led up to the porch that stretched across the front wall and was just wide enough for the rocking chair and a boot rack.

There wasn't a railing for Hunter to lean on, but he didn't need one. He stood bold and stoic as he met Noah by the door.

"It's not a good night, Hunter. Go home," Noah barked, pushing past him.

Hunter reached out and grabbed Noah's arm, stopping him. He turned and gave his cousin a look that might have sent him cowering if there was any moonlight to see his face in the dark night.

Hunter's scowl was barely visible in the darkness. "You need to quit bringin' her around here and stay away from her."

Noah's nostrils flared as he gritted his teeth and sucked in heavy breaths. "Go. Home. Hunter."

"This isn't a game!" Hunter shouted. "I know about Nathan Vanderbilt. He's not just trouble. He's a death wish, and if you think you have anything that can stand up to him, you're wrong."

Noah jerked his arm from Hunter's grasp. "I already warned you I'm in a bad mood. Telling me what to do right now isn't too smart."

"This ranch is all we have, and I won't let you ruin it. You can't risk our livelihood just to see her, Noah."

The scar that ran down the side of Hunter's face was a reminder. Blackwater *was* all they had, and Hunter had sacrificed as much as any of them— possibly more.

Noah shook his head. "Well, you can stop worrying now because she's gone. I just left her place, and I told her it's over."

"What?" Hunter questioned.

"My visit with Nathan today backfired. He wouldn't listen to anything I had to say about my feelings for Camille. He made it very clear that his threat to the ranch still stands. So, I ended things with her."

Hunter didn't react as he let his hand rest by his side. Squaring his shoulders, he said, "You did the right thing."

Noah stepped past him without saying anything and closed himself inside the small cabin he called home. He'd just lost his best friend and the woman he loved, and he wasn't sure he knew what home was anymore.

CHAPTER 28
NOAH

Noah drove through the gates at Blackwater Ranch in a daze. His shift at the fire station had started the morning after he'd gone to Camille's, and it had been a long two days.

His shifts were always tiring, but this time he hadn't been able to sleep or eat like he should to keep his energy up. Losing Camille felt like a constant, nagging hunger. His insides were empty, but he couldn't get filled.

He'd been praying, but no answers had come. Was he supposed to fix this on his own or wait for the Lord to show him how to mend his broken heart?

He topped the slight hill before the main house, and a sinking feeling hit him in the chest. There weren't any trucks parked out front. It was breakfast time. Everyone should've been there.

Noah hastily parked by the door and ran inside, forgetting to take off his shoes.

"Mom. Dad," Noah hollered into the empty dining room.

His mom stepped out of the kitchen and wiped her hands on her apron. "They're all out," his mom said in a shaky voice.

"Where? What happened?"

Worry lines creased her forehead as she reached for his hands. "Someone shot a dozen head of cattle last night."

"A dozen?" They were down twelve cows. That would skew every number they'd banked on for this year. "They were shot? Are you sure?"

The door crashed open, and Micah walked in. His stern face blanketed in concern. "We got another one." He removed his hat and wiped his brow with the back of his hand. "Good. You're here. Where's Lucas?"

"On his way. He stopped at the feed and seed."

"What about Jameson?" Micah asked.

"I'll call both of them on my way to the cabin. I need to get my boots. Pick me up there."

Micah filled his thermos with water at the tap and nodded.

Noah was able to get in touch with Jameson, but Lucas hadn't answered. He'd have to settle for a voicemail and hope his brother hadn't made any extra stops in town.

When Noah was dressed in his T-shirt, boots, and hat, he stepped out onto the porch just as Micah was pulling up. The mid-summer heat was sweltering for once. He was already sweating through his shirt.

Noah jumped in and asked, "What's the plan?"

Micah shifted into gear and shook his head. "We can't bury them. We don't have time, and the wild dogs or wolves will dig 'em up. Most of them are too close to the trees on the east side to burn, and the rendering plant can't get out here for a few more days. The wolves will be all over them by then."

"We can't let that happen." If a pack got a taste of blood, they wouldn't stop there. They would be back day after day picking off the herds. Letting them have even one was like rounding up their meals for the next month.

"We're moving some with the tractor, while Asher and Hunter get the rest of them tied up and ready so when we get to 'em, we can just hook them up.

"And you're sure they were shot?" The question hung in the air for a moment between them before Noah explained. "I broke up with her a few days ago, I swear. You have to believe me."

"I heard, but we still have dead cows. If it's not Nathan, then who is it?"

Nathan wouldn't have done the shooting himself. He'd surely hired someone. Maybe it was already meant to happen before Noah had broken things off with Camille.

What if Nathan knew Noah had gone to Camille's the night he'd broken things off with her and assumed it was something different? Was that what this was about?

"Did you get a bullet out of any of them? Can we have it tested and traced?" Noah asked.

"We did, but I don't know how much good it'll do. Nathan could've paid anyone to take out the cows."

Micah was right. They were helpless when no authority in town would stand up to the Vanderbilt family.

Asher and Hunter had just finished tying up the cow that lay lifeless on its side near the tree line when Noah and Micah pulled up. Aaron was positioning the tractor to hook up to the chains. Nathan had no idea that his daughter loved these animals. She named them and waved at them from the truck when she helped him in the fields. She would be devastated.

Noah jumped out of the truck ready to operate the tractor.

Hunter approached Noah with a look meant to kill. "I thought you said you got rid of her!"

"I did." Noah threw his hands out.

Hunter pointed at the cow. "These were shot.

Not eaten. Somebody did this intentionally, and we don't have any other enemies."

"I get it, but I cut my ties with her the night you came to my place. I haven't spoken to her since."

Hunter's frown was deep and threatening. "We can't lose any more cows. You better make sure he knows you're not hangin' around her no more."

Micah's authoritative voice filled the air. "That's enough. Let's get to work. The predators will smell it soon."

Hunter, Asher, and Aaron stalked off for their truck, while Noah took his place on the tractor.

Hunter was right. If Noah was going to stop this, he needed to make sure that Nathan knew he wasn't seeing Camille anymore.

Nathan had been serious when he said he'd ruin Blackwater. A cut like this could do it already, and they wouldn't survive another hit. They had livestock insurance, but with twelve cows shot, he wasn't sure the insurance company would just pay that money out without asking questions.

What would Camille say if she knew? He couldn't tell her, though. Not when it was her family causing the carnage at the ranch. It would most certainly turn her away from her family, and Noah didn't want to be responsible for that break.

No, Nathan was the one driving a wedge between himself and his own family. Noah wasn't the one killing cattle that put food on the table for a dozen people on this ranch.

Noah loved Camille with all of his heart, but he didn't want to ask her to choose between him and her family. He couldn't. It was selfish of him to ask her to make that choice, especially when it meant losing the ranch to have her. Where would they even live? They couldn't keep the land if they couldn't afford to keep it up.

Camille would find out about this anyway. Someone would tell her. It's a small town.

Noah shifted the gears on the tractor. Sweat dripped down his temple, and he wasn't sure if it was the heat or the indecision in his heart. He inched the tractor forward to make sure the chains would catch, but they didn't. Micah was standing by the truck on his phone probably figuring out where they were needed next.

Jumping off the tractor, Noah's phone vibrated in his pocket. When he slipped it out, his breath hung in his throat. Camille's name and a photo of her wearing her new cowboy hat lit up the screen.

Looking back at Micah, he realized he probably had a few minutes before they had to start dragging. He'd ignored her enough the last time he'd cut things off with her because of Nathan, but it didn't seem fair to do that to her again. The last thing he wanted to do was ignore her, and answering her call would be so easy. He wanted to hear her voice badly enough that Nathan's threats seemed far away.

"Hello."

"Hey. Is this a bad time? I thought we could talk."

Noah glanced over his shoulder at Micah and stepped a few paces toward the woods. "I have a few minutes to spare. I might have to let you go soon."

Camille sighed, creating a static sound on the phone. "I just don't understand. I felt like things were fine, and it's hard to wrap my mind around how you could tell me you love me one morning and break up with me that evening."

Noah used the heel of his boot to dig up a thistle at the foot of a tree. She was right. He had told her he loved her that morning and meant it. He still did.

Camille went on, "I love you, and I don't want us to be apart. If there's something weighing on you, just talk to me about it. I told you that you could confide in me about anything. Even if it's Nathan, like I think it is."

She'd been his best friend for as long as he could remember. If there was anyone he could talk to, it should've been her. But this situation was different.

He wanted to say something, but words wouldn't come. Taking his cowboy hat off, he wiped the sweat on his head with his sleeve.

Noah was still throwing words around in his head that might make sense when he heard a fallen branch snap and locked eyes with a predator. He froze as a full-grown brown bear lifted one paw to move closer to him. The bear was so close he could smell its damp fur.

Camille's voice was in his ear. "Noah, I want you to know I'm here."

He knew not to run, but he was standing between a grizzly and the fresh blood it smelled.

Noah whispered, "I have to go. There's a bear—"

"A bear!" Camille yelled. "Where are you?"

The bear was less than ten feet from him and advancing slowly as if it knew this hunt was over. Noah kept his eyes on the bear and took one step back before the bear charged.

CHAPTER 29
NOAH

Noah tried to hold his ground, but the bear was running toward him now. He lowered the phone from his ear and yelled, "Micah!"

He took two steps backward on instinct. He wasn't running, but he was pretty sure it was the better option right now.

On the third step back, his heel snagged on a fallen branch. He fell backward, arms flailing, and his phone went soaring through the air.

"Micah!" Noah couldn't take his eyes off the advancing predator to see if his brother was coming to help, but he prayed he'd yelled loud enough to be heard over the running tractor.

The bear slowed as it approached Noah lying on his back. The fall had knocked the wind out of him, but he wasn't breathing anyway. The bear's large paw lifted and swiped down faster than any animal that large should've been able to move.

Noah cried out once more as the claws sliced across his thigh. "Micah!"

A boom filled the air, followed by another, and the bear jerked backward and fell onto its side.

Noah could hear Micah running toward him as another shot rang through the air, but the bear was lumbering into the thick trees with a wounded cry.

Micah stopped running when he reached Noah and scanned the woods.

"I think he's gone," Noah moaned.

Micah crouched beside him, panting. "He might be back. I didn't hit a kill shot."

They both knew there could be hefty fines for killing a grizzly in these parts. That was another financial burden to add to their list.

Micah dropped the gun and wrangled his phone from his pocket. Dialing, he asked Noah, "What do I do?"

Noah looked down at his leg for the first time. His jeans were shredded and covered in blood. The slices were deep and gaping. He couldn't even feel it yet. The shock was too great. "Call Lucas."

"I am."

Noah took a deep breath in through his nose and blew out through his mouth. Steadying his heart rate was vital right now. He could bleed out quickly this far from medical help. "Tell him to bring my bag from the closet in the main house. He knows where it is."

Micah was talking to Lucas now and relayed Noah's instructions.

"Get an ambulance out here." Noah sucked in a breath through gritted teeth. "They can meet us at the main house."

Micah's face was ghostly white as he hung up the call. "Lucas said Camille is at the main house. She was telling them something was wrong when I called."

"What? I was just on the phone with her."

She hadn't said she was on her way to the ranch, but their conversation hadn't gotten far.

Micah eyed the wounds. "They're on their way, and they're bringing the new truck. It'll be an easier ride for you with more room. What can I do until then?"

"Who? You said 'they.'"

"I don't know. Lucas just said we'll be there in a few."

He prayed Camille wasn't coming out here. The bear might still be hanging around, and he didn't want Camille anywhere near here."

"What can I do?" Micah repeated.

"Nothing. I want my supplies before I try to move. Lucas can help me if I can't finish it." Noah could feel his head getting lighter and the dizziness was starting. The pain arrived like a gust of summer wind, and Noah gritted his teeth. He had to stay conscious until Lucas got here and Noah could tell his brother what to do.

Noah was fighting the darkness when the truck pulled up. Lucas jumped out with his dad and Camille. The three of them ran toward him, but Camille and Silas stayed back, while Noah pointed to various supplies in the bag and instructed Lucas on what to do.

Lucas cut open Noah's pants leg and bandaged the wound enough to move him. Then Lucas, Micah, and Silas carried him as gently as they could to the bed of the truck.

Camille and Lucas jumped into the back with him as the others filed into the cab.

"What are you doing here?" Noah asked her as she rested his head in her lap. The blinding sun was high in the sky now, and he couldn't open his eyes to look at her.

"I was already on my way here when I called you. I wanted to see you. And when you said there was a bear, I panicked." She stroked his sweaty cheek as the truck bumped over the uneven terrain and he winced from the pain. "I ran in and told your mom and Lucas that we needed to find you because something was wrong."

"You shouldn't have come out here." His brain wasn't working right, and he wasn't sure what he'd been meaning to say.

"Hush. I'm here now."

Camille was here, and he focused on the feel of her delicate hands stroking his face and not Lucas's assessment of his shredded leg. If he thought about the fire that burned there, he would scream.

His nostrils flared as he forced his breaths in and out. *Don't think. Don't think.*

He heard Camille mumbling a prayer above him, and he whispered, "I'm glad you're here," before the darkness consumed him.

CHAPTER 30
CAMILLE

She couldn't lose him. Not again, and not like this.

Camille raked her hands through Noah's hair while his head lay in her lap. She was trying to be brave. It wouldn't do either of them any good to break apart right now. Noah needed her to stay alert and strong for him.

"I'm glad you're here."

His words were faint, but she'd heard him. Whatever reason he had for breaking up with her didn't matter now. A tear slid down her face as she prayed.

"Lord, please lay Your hand on Noah. Help us get him to the help he needs in time. Help me to be strong. Help us." Her words cracked at the end, and she squeezed her eyes closed. "Please, Lord. I don't want to lose him."

Tears burned her eyes when she opened them. He was lying still—too still.

She looked to Lucas. "I think he's unconscious!"

Lucas held the injured leg stationary. "Almost there."

She turned and stretched her neck to see the main house over the next rise. The red-and-white ambulance was parked in front.

The paramedics carefully moved him out of the bed of the truck and onto a gurney, while Camille helplessly watched them take over his care. Noah's mom and the rest of his family waited nearby. Camille rushed to Anita and hugged her neck.

"It's okay," Camille said with compassion. "He's gonna be okay."

Noah's mom rubbed Camille's back. "I know, baby. He's a tough one just like all my boys."

She couldn't imagine what Anita had gone through raising five boys. Camille's memory had flourished and opened more in the last few weeks at Blackwater Ranch than in the whole six months before, and she remembered at least a handful of times when the Harding boys had narrowly escaped death.

When Noah was loaded into the ambulance, Camille stepped back and gestured for Anita to go with him.

Mama Harding just patted Camille's hand. "You go. I'll ride with Silas, and we'll meet you there."

Camille nodded and climbed into the back of the ambulance. The medic was assessing Noah's vitals efficiently.

"I'm Camille."

The man had dark skin the color of pine bark and bright green friendly eyes. "Travis. I'm not in Noah's crew, but I'm his relief at the station."

"So, you know him?"

"Oh, yeah."

"Is he gonna be okay?"

Travis' gaze darted to various machines and over Noah's leg. "That's the hope."

Camille held Noah's hand in hers and knew this couldn't be the end. She'd just gotten him back, and the thought of losing him made her want to retch. She could touch him. He was here now. He couldn't be taken away.

But she knew he could if the Lord willed it. If there wasn't anything the medical professionals could do to help, then this might be her last day with him.

They arrived at Cody Memorial Hospital, and Camille stayed out of the way as they moved him inside. She followed them as far as they'd let her. One kind nurse had directed her to the closest waiting room where she'd called Anita to let her know where to go.

The waiting room was eerily quiet. No one else

was around, and few people even walked by the window. She was too alone with her thoughts.

A bear! She knew Noah always carried a weapon out on the ranch, but an actual attack seemed like something she never thought would happen to anyone at Blackwater.

Camille was pacing the floor when Anita came in.

"Have you heard anything?" Anita was about five steps ahead of Silas and Lucas.

"No, but they said they'd come find us when he got settled or if there was news."

Silas laid a hand on Anita's shoulder, and she turned to tuck herself under his protective wing. "Our job now is to wait and pray," he declared.

Camille let out a heavy sigh. Noah's dad was right. She could do that. She just needed to calm her heart until they heard from the doctor.

Camille and Noah's family stood when a nurse entered the waiting room.

"Harding family?"

"Yes," they all said in unison.

Camille wasn't actually family, but she sure felt like it after all that had happened between them.

She'd spent years with Noah on the other side of her injury and weeks on this side, but they felt even.

They'd finally moved into a relationship, and they'd been comfortable there until a few days ago.

The nurse waved them toward her. "You can see him now. He's doing great."

"He's awake?" Anita asked.

"He is. Didn't take him long. Unfortunately, he was awake for the stitching. Inside and out."

Camille's stomach turned at the thought of stitching up the long, deep wounds she'd seen. She still had his blood on her shirt and jeans.

They were following the nurse down the sterile hallway when footsteps bounded up behind them. Turning, Camille saw Micah jogging to catch them.

"Wait up."

Silas clapped a heavy hand on his son's shoulder. "You get 'em taken care of?"

"Yeah, we drug 'em all to the southern pasture, and Hunter is in charge."

"Good work, son."

Anita and Silas stepped into the room first, and Camille hung back.

Micah gestured for her to go in ahead of him, but she held up her hand.

"I'll just let family go first."

Micah tilted his chin toward the door and gave her a sad look. "You did good today, Millie. Go on in and see him."

Each of Noah's brothers had treated her differently. Some were friendly and went out of their way to make her feel welcome, while others like Aaron and Hunter avoided her. She tried not to let it bother her, thinking maybe there was something in their past that might keep them at a distance.

Micah hadn't ever really said much to her at all. Now, she was beginning to wonder if he was actually on team Millie.

"Thanks. I'm really glad you were with him. Did you... how did you get the bear off him?"

Micah shoved his hands in his pockets. "I shot it."

Killing a grizzly could come with consequences. She didn't know if defense changed the punishment, but the thought didn't sit well with her. "Did you kill it?"

He huffed. "I don't know. Thankfully, it didn't come back."

Camille nodded, eyes wide. "Agreed."

Micah gave her a lazy side smile as he nudged her shoulder. "Get in there."

She stepped slowly into the room, afraid of what she might find. When she saw Noah sitting on the bed, he looked almost normal, except for the drab hospital gown. His color was pale, and there were dark patches beneath his eyes, but he was smiling. That smile lifted her heart, and she said a powerful prayer of thanks in that moment.

Noah extended his hand to her. "You stayed."

"Of course I stayed!" She didn't care that his

family was in the room. She ran to him and hugged him gently without sabotaging the wires and tubes connected to him.

She whispered into his hair, "I was terrified."

"Don't be scared. Everything is fine."

When she pulled back, Noah's face was grave. "I can't believe you came out there knowing there was a bear around. Why did Lucas bring you?"

"Because I told him I was going, whether I rode with him or drove myself. He didn't have much choice." She shrugged and lifted her brows.

"What if the bear had come back? I wasn't in any shape to protect you."

Camille brushed his hair from his face. "I didn't know if I could be much help, but I had to go to you. It was like a part of myself was in trouble." She lowered her voice as Noah's family spoke in hushed voices on the other side of the room. "I love you, and I couldn't stay back wondering if you were okay or not."

Noah pulled her closer to him and buried his face in her neck. "You were brave. Braver than I've been lately. And you've already saved me. But please don't run toward danger, even if I'm there."

"Then don't scare me like that again!"

Noah lifted his head to look at her but kept his arm around her waist. "Not many people have someone in their life who would run into danger to help them." He tightened his grip on her. "I should've fought harder for us."

"What happened?" she asked tentatively.

"I was giving up on us hoping that no one would get hurt, but it didn't help." Noah looked at his family as they stared back at him, confirming that they knew all about the breakup and why.

"Anyone want to tell me a story?" Camille quizzed.

Micah cleared his throat. "Someone shot a dozen cows last night."

"What?" she shrieked. After the auction she'd gone to with Noah a few weeks ago, she knew that each cow could cost thousands of dollars. If they lost a dozen, that could cripple the ranch.

When no one would look at her, she turned to Noah. "Who?"

Noah was biting the inside of his cheek and twisting the bedsheet in his hand. "We think it was Nathan."

"You knew this was coming, didn't you? It's because of us."

Noah nodded.

Camille's anger boiled inside her. She'd hoped and pretended that Nathan wasn't capable of something so horrible, but she was having a hard time denying the evidence before her.

"And what were you doing when the bear attacked you?" she asked Noah.

Micah answered for him. "Dragging the cows away from the edge of the property so the predators wouldn't get them."

Camille's chest rose and fell in deep pulses. How could Nathan do this? No one here could answer that question, but she was about to find out for herself.

"I think I need to talk to someone. I'll be back in a little while."

Noah reached out to stop her. "No, Millie. I already talked to him. That's what started all this."

"What do you mean?"

"I went to see him the other night before I came to your place. I wanted to explain how much you mean to me and that I could provide a good life for you. But he isn't going to change his mind about us. He reminded me that I would never be good enough for a Vanderbilt. He also promised that if I didn't back off, he'd ruin the ranch and take everything we have. I don't think there's anything we can say to him to make him listen."

Camille turned to Noah's family. These people meant the world to her, and she couldn't just stand here while they worried, suffered, and bled for no good reason.

"I have to try, Noah. We have to find a way. I won't accept any other outcome."

"I don't want to be the one who hurts your family," he pleaded. "Your mom doesn't know."

Camille shook her head. "She'll know before the day is over. She has a right to know about the man she's married to."

Noah let his hand fall from her arm. "I can't stop you if it's what you want to do, but know that it might not change things. He's well on his way to taking everything."

Camille nodded and kissed his forehead. He was dirty and sweaty, but she didn't care. Her love saw past the dirt.

"I'll be back really soon. Just rest." Then she leaned in to whisper in his ear, "I love you."

She said her good-byes to his family and kept her emotions in check as she exited the hospital. But inside, she was screaming.

CHAPTER 31

CAMILLE

Her foot rested heavy on the accelerator as she drove from Cody to Blackwater. Anger and betrayal built within her with every mile that passed beneath her tires.

Twisting her hands on the steering wheel, she ached for a distraction. Something to calm the storm of her emotions. *How could Nathan do something so horrible?*

She called Jenny and let the ringing in her car speakers drown out the roiling in her ears.

"Hey. What's up?"

"Noah is in the hospital in Cody. A bear attacked him this morning."

"What?" Jenny screamed. "Is he okay?"

Camille's voice shook. "He is now. It looked so bad after it happened, though. It clawed his leg up good."

Rustling sounded on Jenny's end of the line. "Do I need to come?"

"No," Camille assured her. "He's doing okay. They stitched him up and he's conscious now, but he lost a lot of blood. He'll be in quite a bit of pain while it heals."

"I can't imagine."

"They were cleaning up a dozen cows that were shot last night when the bear attacked." Camille's tone grew higher in pitch. "Can you imagine this? They think Nathan shot them... or had someone else do it."

Jenny was quiet for a heartbeat, and her tone was grave when she spoke. "Are they sure?"

"No, but I'm about to find out. Could he really have done this?"

"It's possible. The Vanderbilt name means everything to him. I've heard some terrible things about how he's abused the power of a founding family from people in town, but he's never shown that side of himself around us. It's hard to say. Do they have any proof? Are they going to investigate?"

"Micah said they have a bullet, but it'll be hard to prove it's him. Especially if he hired someone. Who in town would go against Nathan Vanderbilt?"

"You're right," Jenny conceded. "Blackwater Ranch might not make it through this."

Camille took a deep breath to calm her racing heart. "A dozen cattle lost, a possible fine or worse for killing a grizzly, Noah's leg is mutilated, and he probably won't be able to work at the ranch or the fire station for a while."

"I think I'm going to be sick," Jenny choked. "The Hardings didn't deserve this."

"No, they definitely didn't! And I'm about to find out for myself if Nathan is behind it. Although, expecting honesty from someone capable of something like this is farfetched."

"Be careful, Millie. If he doesn't care about taking everything from an innocent family, I don't want to think about what he's capable of."

"I love you, Jenny. Please pray," Camille asked.

"Of course. I love you too."

Camille ended the call feeling better knowing at least someone else was praying for a positive outcome of this meeting. She couldn't fix what had already been done, but maybe she could prevent Nathan from doing any more awful things to the Harding family.

She parked in front of her parents' house and prayed as she walked to the door. The only one capable of calming her heart right now was the Lord.

The front door stayed locked, and she hadn't called ahead to let anyone know she was coming. Fumbling a dozen keys on her keyring, she looked for the purple one her mother had labeled *Home* after her wreck. It had taken them weeks to label all of them.

She pushed the door open to the elaborate home they'd moved into when Camille was twelve years old. The place had never felt like home to her, probably because it was too grand and pristine. Camille searched the main rooms before finding her mother in the kitchen.

Bonnie Vanderbilt looked like a Stepford wife with her gently curling hair and summer dress.

"Baby! I didn't know you were coming." Her mother laid the paint swatches in her hand on the table and ushered Camille in, hugging her tight. "I wish you stopped by more often."

"I'm sorry, Mom." Camille knew she really should try to spend more time with her mother. "I'm actually looking for Nathan." Camille's anger had cooled slightly at meeting her mother's sunny disposition.

"Oh, he's in the study." Her mother pulled away from their hug and gasped. "What's all over you?"

The blood. Noah's blood. The splotches were scattered over her clothes. Camille's voice shook. "I need to see Nathan."

"Are you hurt?"

"No, Mom, but this is important."

"Come on." Her mother led her to the study and gestured for her to enter first.

When she walked through the doorway and saw

him sitting at his desk, she doubted the man could have killed a dozen cows at Blackwater Ranch. His salt-and-pepper hair was tidy, and his thin-framed glasses sat studiously on the bridge of his nose.

Her mom knocked twice on the open door and hurriedly said, "Honey, Camille is here."

When Nathan lifted his head, the innocent features faded into one of guilt, and she knew he'd done it.

Camille stepped forward, keeping her gaze locked on his. He didn't greet her. He knew why she was here.

"Did you do it?"

Nathan stood. It was a subtle power play. He wouldn't be caught lazing during the upcoming battle.

"Did he do what?" her mother asked frantically.

Camille clarified, "Did you kill the livestock at Blackwater Ranch?"

Her mother's sharp intake of breath behind her wasn't a surprise.

"I'm not asking if you did it personally," Camille said. "I know you weren't out in the woods last night picking off cows. I'm asking you if you hired someone to ruin everything that the Hardings have been working to keep profitable for generations."

Nathan hadn't moved, and blood pulsed loudly in Camille's ears.

"Nathan?" Her mother's sweet voice pleaded for him to deny it.

"Silence speaks a thousand words," she said, walking closer. "How could you?" Camille screamed when his continued silence verified his guilt.

She wanted him to vehemently deny it. She wanted him to move around the desk and hug her with assurances that he hadn't known about this and he wasn't trying to ruin the lives of the people she loved.

"Why would you do this?" Camille asked.

Finally, Nathan spoke, and his words mirrored the anger she felt. "Because he's not good enough for you!" His deep voice echoed in the room, and his hand gestured wildly in his explanation. "Because if you tied yourself to him, he'd drag you down to his level and you'd be no better than him and his family of farmers! Because I know what's best for you, and the Vanderbilt name is worthy of a marriage to a prestigious family!"

The purple veins protruding from Nathan's red face didn't scare her. She stepped closer to the desk that separated them and steadied her words.

"Do you have any idea what you've done? Oh, you killed the cows all right—the lifeblood of that land and the people who live on it—but you almost killed Noah today, too."

Her mother stepped up beside her and grabbed her hand. "Is he all right? What happened?"

Camille couldn't spare a glance for her mother right now. Nathan's face had shown a flicker of shock before returning to its scowl.

"He's being treated at Cody Memorial right now. He was trying to clean up the mess you made before the predators invaded. A bear attacked him and shredded his leg."

The fresh memory of the blood that had drenched him flooded her mind. The metallic smell had been overwhelming, even in the open air.

She pointed to her bloodstained shirt. "This is his. A bear attacked him while he was trying to salvage what's left of the ranch! Do you hear me? These are innocent people's lives you're ruining. A kid lives on that ranch! If they can't keep the ranch, they'll all be homeless!"

Nathan squared his shoulders and furrowed his brow. "If you'd been smart enough to hang around with the right people, none of this would've happened."

Camille stopped and became unexpectedly calm before continuing. "Noah and his family are good people. You don't know anything about them because they're not good enough in your eyes. I don't care about the money in his pocket, and I think you forget that I'm an adult who can make her own decisions. You have no right to think you can decide who I love. And just so we're clear, it'll always be Noah." She leaned in closer, gritting out her next words and pointing a finger at him. "Nothing you do will ever change that. If you bankrupt that ranch, you'll be sealing my fate too. I'm tied to that ranch more than I'm tied to the Vanderbilt name. And I'll choose to stand beside Noah through anything."

Tears were running down Camille's face now, but they were born of anger. "The man I love fought tooth and nail and sacrificed everything to protect that land, and I can't do anything but admire his loyalty to his family and their way of life. That's something I'll never be able to say about you. I love Noah, and he doesn't deserve to be threatened and ruined for loving me!"

Her mother stepped forward beside her, and Camille's attention was drawn to the stoic resolve in her mother's posture. She'd never seen her mother so serious and bold as she glared at Nathan.

Bonnie's voice was calm and sure as she asked her husband, "How could you do something like this after what you went through?"

Nathan's lips pursed, and Camille wasn't sure he was breathing as his gaze was locked on her mother.

"You think that a last name is what saved you? You're so wrong," Bonnie said. "Your parents might not have been the most caring, but they were selfless enough to take in a poor young boy when he needed the help they could provide."

What was her mother talking about? A poor

boy? What had Grandma and Grandpa Vanderbilt done?

Her mother continued. "Their money didn't save you—their kindness and selflessness did. I don't think you ever understood that."

"The money came with the name, Bonnie! The money fed me, the money clothed me, and the money healed me, but the money came from the name!"

"No, money can't save anyone. Kindness saves people, and you're too proud of your name to realize that. Noah saved Camille's life. Did that mean nothing to you? You can't see past Noah's job and be grateful for what he's given us."

Her mother turned toward Camille and brushed a delicate hand down her hair. "He gave me more days with my baby, and I've thanked God for him every day."

Her mom turned back to Nathan. "But he was good for Camille before he saved her. I bet you were the one who sent him away when she left for college."

Nathan stood silent for a moment. He was outnumbered, but he would go down swinging. "He kidnapped her and took her to Colorado! She was a child."

"Exactly. They were young and stupid, but had either of them ever done anything destructive before? Have they done anything like that since? It was out of character, and we both know Camille and Noah have good heads on their shoulders. I don't ever worry about her falling into bad decisions. I trust her, and I know that if she loves Noah, it's because he's good for her."

Nathan huffed and threw his hands in the air. "Neither of you understand the work I put in to keep our family at the top."

"I don't care about being at the top," Bonnie said. "I care about what you've done to that family. I'm appalled that the man I married and love is capable of something so terrible."

Nathan's resolve faltered. "Bonnie, we just need to talk about this."

"I'm finished talking," Camille said. "I need to change clothes and get back to the hospital."

Her mother rested a hand on her shoulder and guided her toward the door. "I'll drive you. You must be shaken up."

"Bonnie, wait," Nathan pleaded. "Camille."

Camille turned around. "I don't have anything else to say to you. I trusted you, and look at what you've done. I've lost all respect for you."

Nathan gasped and his chest rose and fell quickly. Panic laced his tone as he said, "Bonnie?"

"I'm driving my daughter to the hospital to check on Noah, and we have a lot to talk about when I return."

The resolve in her mother's voice threaded into

Camille's skin. Bonnie Vanderbilt was a force to be reckoned with when she'd been deceived.

Camille and her mother left Nathan's study and didn't speak until they were in the car. Having her rock beside her gave Camille the strength to face the situation and whatever might be waiting for them at the hospital.

When they were settled into the drive, Bonnie whispered, "I'd like to pray for Noah and his family."

Camille reached for her mother's hand. "Please." They needed every prayer now because Noah wasn't completely out of the woods just yet. He had a long recovery ahead of him, and Camille intended to be right beside him helping every step of the way.

CHAPTER 32
CAMILLE

"There's a lot you don't know about Nathan, but none of it excuses what he did," Bonnie said.

Bonnie went with Camille to her house to change clothes and pack a bag of extras, in case Noah stayed at the hospital overnight. She planned on staying there until he came home. She'd called Anita and rounded up some things she needed too. Now, Camille and her mom were back on the road, and they had a lot to talk about.

"Nathan was adopted when he was four years old," Bonnie began. "He was neglected as a child, and he had a handful of health problems that had never been treated. By the time he was taken from his parents, he was malnourished, dehydrated, and had several broken bones and bruises."

Camille turned away from her mother. She

244MANDI BLAKE

wasn't sure if she'd ever heard this story before, but her heart told her she hadn't.

"Your grandparents didn't have any children, but they had been in touch with the local foster care system and were contacted when Nathan was still recovering. They adopted him."

So, Nathan technically wasn't a true Vanderbilt, and Camille felt sorry for him. "That's exactly why I wanted to practice family law, Mom. I want to help kids like that find families who will love them. Why did he push me in a different direction?"

"Because he didn't want you to see the worst of this world. He's been through it and almost didn't make it." Bonnie swallowed hard and stared at the road ahead. "I can't believe he did this."

"I can't either. I love Noah, and he's a good man. He's someone Nathan should want me to be with." Camille squeezed her mother's hand. "Noah would be a great husband."

"Honey, I know. You don't have to tell me twice. I always knew Nathan didn't like Noah, but he always downplayed his dislike around me and changed the subject. I never knew he was so adamant about your relationship with Noah."

They pulled into the parking lot at Cody Memorial, and Bonnie parked the car. Turning toward each other, they both grinned. Camille would bet that their smiles were mirror images of each other. She had her mom's shapely lips and bright-green eyes, while her straight nose and pointed chin came from her dad.

"I love you, baby."

"I'm sorry about all this, Mom."

Her mom turned and squared her shoulders. "Oh, this isn't your fault. Had I known, I would've told you to stick with Noah regardless of what Nathan said."

"I didn't even know any of this until today. I suspected some things, but I never knew for sure."

Her mother sighed. "I'm sorry I didn't figure this out sooner... before anyone got hurt."

"No, none of this is your fault," Camille said. "Nathan is the only one to blame."

Bonnie patted her hand. "You're right. Let's go check on Noah."

Before knocking on his door, they checked with the nurse's station to make sure he hadn't been moved.

Upon entering, Noah's mother lay reclined in a chair in the corner of the room. The lights were off, but a dim glow shone through the closed blinds of the window. Noah lay sleeping on the bed while monitors quietly recorded his vitals.

Anita righted herself and rose from the chair. "Bonnie?"

Camille's mother stepped quietly into the room and whispered, "I'm so sorry, Anita. How is he?"

Anita waved her hand between them before

clasping Bonnie's like an old friend. "Oh, you don't have to whisper. He's sound asleep. The nurses have been in here poking and prodding on him, and he didn't stir. They say he's doing fine. The recovery will be long and painful, but they don't anticipate any complications." She nodded her chin toward the various tubes and wires. "They said the antibiotic they have him on should keep away any infection."

Bonnie shook her head. "I can't take back what's been done to him, but please know that I had nothing to do with this."

"I know you didn't," Anita confirmed. "Noah warned us something might be coming if he didn't stop seeing Camille, and we prepared for the worst. We had some savings put back in case this happened."

"Anita, I will reimburse you every penny you lost and more. Don't doubt that. We'll talk later, and you can let me know what you need."

"I appreciate that. We have livestock insurance, but they haven't gotten back to us about the claim yet. They might not pay it without an investigation." Anita shook her head. "I'm sorry. I don't mean to burden you with our problems. It's nice to have you here."

Camille moved to Noah's side while their mothers talked. She hated seeing him like this, but at least he wasn't in pain while he slept. She didn't want to wake him, but she ached to touch him, if only to let him know she was there beside him... every step of the way.

She would stand with him through this. He would need her help now more than ever, and after all he'd done to help her recover these past few months, she wanted to repay his kindness.

Anita and Bonnie stepped out, leaving Camille alone with him. He opened his eyes half an hour later and gave her a lazy smile.

She touched his hand then—a show of solidarity, no matter what came next.

They were meant to save each other in different ways and in different times. What she had with Noah was rare, and she knew enough to hold onto something precious when she found it.

"Hey," she whispered.

"Hey, yourself. How long have you been here?"

She shrugged. "I got back about an hour or so ago."

Noah blinked a few times and shook his head as if to clear a fog. "What happened? He didn't..."

"No, I'm fine." Grasping his hand, she gave him a half grin. "I'm not sure how much good I did, but I gave him a piece of my mind. Mom knows now, too, and she's fit to be tied."

Noah rested his head back and closed his eyes. "I should've done something sooner."

"I'm glad you didn't try to take him on back then. No one had the resources or the manpower to protect the ranch, and everything might have crumbled."

"What do we have now?" he asked.

"Hope. We just have to hope and pray that he comes around. Mom already said she'd reimburse the ranch for the cattle, and I'm sure she'll be paying your hospital bills too. She feels awful for not seeing through Nathan sooner, and so do I."

Noah's deep voice was soft and tired as he said, "No, I should've just told you. I just didn't want to cause a rift in your family."

"Nathan did that on his own." She brushed his hair from his face. "It'll always be you and me. I'll be right here, no matter what comes next. We'll face it together, and we'll be better for it."

"I know you're right about how we shouldn't have tried to stand up to him when we were young, but I missed a lot of years with you."

Camille smiled. "You're stuck with me now. There's lots of time to make up for them."

Noah nodded, and his dark eyes were gentle and knowing. "I'll hold you to it."

CHAPTER 33
NOAH

Camille glanced over both shoulders as if checking to make sure the coast was clear before extending both hands, palms up, toward Sprite. "Take your pick, pretty lady." One hand offered an apple and the other a sugar cube.

Noah wasn't sure who liked treat time the most, his girlfriend or the horse. Dixie circled Camille's legs, begging for attention. He'd just watched from the tailgate as Camille rode Sprite through the pasture by the stable.

"Sugar. Always a good choice." Camille waited for the blue roan to finish the treats before nuzzling noses with the big softie.

It'd been a week since Noah was released from the hospital, and he was still getting used to needing help completing small tasks. The bandages were cumbersome and needed to be changed often.

Not to mention small things like showering and putting on pants had become a chore.

Camille spent every moment she could helping him. He didn't mind it when she helped, but it was an unspoken truth that any "help" from his brothers was unwelcome. He'd have to be wheelchair bound before he'd let another man help him up the three steps leading into the main house. Three times a day, he nodded a greeting to his brothers as they passed him and his crutches on the way to meals.

No one had heard from Nathan since the day of the bear attack. Camille still spoke to her mother regularly, but Bonnie had left to visit her sister in Montana the day after the attack. Camille said her mother needed time to come to terms with what had happened, and Noah understood. He wasn't sure how he'd feel after finding out the person he was married to had done what Nathan had.

True to her nature, Camille was putting on a brave face. He'd seen the same masking of her fear during the earlier stages of her recovery. Two creases would deepen between her brows and she'd bite the inside of her lip while working on some chore around the ranch, and he knew she was worried.

She'd waded through a time in her life full of unanswered questions only to be greeted with a betrayal by someone she thought she could trust. Loyalty was important to Camille. It always had been. He often thought that was the biggest reason Camille had tied herself to him all those years ago. He'd let her know then that he would stand beside her every chance he got, and it had been the biggest break in his character when he'd broken ties with her when she'd moved to Portland.

At least she still had Jenny. Talking to her mom on the phone was one thing, but being able to actually see Jenny and talk through things with her had done wonders for Camille's spirits after the incident. The men at the ranch weren't much to talk to. His mom was great for advice or small talk if you were willing to work beside her in the kitchen, but Camille always found her place beside Noah when she came to the ranch, eager to help if he needed her. She'd even promised to help his mom with the renovations for the upstairs guest rooms the coming weekend. Mom had her heart set on renting out the rooms in the winter, bed and breakfast style.

The sun was beginning to set over the mountains, and the breeze lifted Camille's ponytail as she handed Sprite off to Lucas.

The faint crunching of gravel under tires seeped into the silence of the evening. Dixie lifted her ears, nose pointed toward the noise. Lucas lifted his head as Noah and Camille turned toward the entrance to Blackwater Ranch. A brand new charcoal-gray pickup truck was easing up the dirt path.

"That's Nathan," Camille said. The words were

flat without a hint of the turmoil that undoubtedly churned within her.

Noah reached for his crutches and hoisted himself up. "Let's go. He's headed for the main house."

Whatever Nathan wanted, Noah would be ready. They'd all known there was a possibility that Nathan would try something else, but with Bonnie gone, they didn't have a chance of a warning.

Camille rushed to the truck and opened Noah's door before rushing around to the driver's side. Lucas bolted Sprite in her stall, sprinted from the stable, and climbed into the bed of the truck. At Lucas's double tap on the side of the pickup, Camille jerked the old ranch truck into gear and rumbled one hundred yards down the dirt path to the main house with Dixie keeping pace beside them.

Camille and Lucas jumped out first, then she was helping Noah out before the dust had settled.

Nathan had already parked and gotten out of his truck but stood unhurried beside the driver's door. His hair was longer, and his slacks were wrinkled. The subtle changes were barely noticeable, but Noah had known Nathan Vanderbilt for years. Wrinkles and tousled hair were imperfections that Noah hadn't seen on Camille's stepdad before today.

It was almost imperceptible, but Nathan tensed as the Hardings filed from the truck and the main house. Aaron, Micah, Anita, and Silas stepped outside, while Lucas positioned himself next to Noah's injured side. Camille stood tall on his other side, silent and poised for whatever may come next. Dixie was uncharacteristically calm next to Camille.

"I wasn't expecting an audience for this," Nathan said.

"Why are you here?" Camille asked.

Nathan tucked his chin and took a deep breath. "I'm here to apologize. I have a lot to apologize for, and I know I can't make up for everything in one visit. I'm just here to start." He brushed a hand over his mouth. "I miss you, Camille. That's only one of the reasons why I'm here. I know we've had a rocky relationship since your wreck, but we used to be close. You were my little girl, and I loved watching you grow. You had so much potential, and I just wanted you to take advantage of every opportunity."

Noah wrapped his arm around Camille's shoulder and pulled her in close. Aaron, Micah, and Silas stood on the porch with arms crossed over their chests. Anita wrung her hands in her apron.

"I was wrong," Nathan said in a shaky voice. "I tried to control a part of your life I had no business in." He glanced at Noah for a moment before directing his attention back at Camille. "When you were little, I prayed you would meet a godly man and be happy with him. Then Noah came along, and I worried. He wasn't like us, and he wasn't the man I had in mind for you."

Camille leaned into Noah's side, letting him know where she stood. Beside him, always beside him. Through the good and the bad.

Nathan continued. "I started praying that the Lord would send you someone else. Anyone but him. He didn't really do anything wrong until he took you to Colorado. By then, I was so worried about you, I knew I had to do something to get you away from him. So I told him he had to let you go. He had to let you go to college and make the most of your life because I knew you wouldn't do that if you were tied to him here.

"I was wrong. Your mother—" Nathan swallowed hard and covered his eyes before continuing. "Your mother showed me that I was wrong. She told me I should have confided in her, and she was right. Your mother is patient and understanding, but I'm not those things. I knew she felt differently about you and Noah."

Camille looked at Noah now, and her expression was grave but relaxed. Nathan was apologizing, and this was a huge moment for her. After feeling betrayed, knowing he could come to her like this could mean either closure or healing.

Nathan took one step toward Camille and extended his arms before letting them fall back at his sides. "Our family has always attended church, but I haven't lived the life I should as a Christian. I wasn't living as Christ would have me to, and

Bonnie... she reminded me of how far I'd fallen. I've been a poor father to you lately. I got caught up in the wrong things—money and appearances."

Nathan turned to Noah and took two more steps. "I owe you an apology too. I was blinded by selfishness and pride, and I couldn't see that you're a good man. You're good for her. I've seen how happy you make her, and that's more than I can say about myself. You were there for her when I wasn't."

When Nathan turned to Camille, she straightened her shoulders. Noah knew she would forgive her stepdad. He'd known Camille for a long time, and she wasn't one to give up on someone.

The question was, could Noah forgive too?

Nathan's eyes were wet with tears as he looked at his daughter. "I'm going to try my best to be better for you. I don't expect you to accept my apology or forgive me, but I'll always love you, and I'm sorry for everything that I did."

Before she could respond, Nathan turned to Noah's family standing on the porch. His chin trembled as he spoke. "I owe you an apology too. I took something from you that meant more than money. The worst thing I could've done was take out my anger on innocent people and animals, and I ruthlessly did just that. I know Bonnie has already paid for the lost cattle, but I intend to do more. Silas, Anita, I'd like to speak with you about what I can do to help this ranch. I feel awful for what I've done to you. Please allow me to make up for it."

Silas nodded, and Anita grasped her husband's hand in solidarity.

In that moment, Noah knew he would forgive Nathan. Camille's heart was capable of it, and Noah could move past what had been done if the threats were removed. All he'd ever wanted was to be able to love Camille and work the ranch in peace. With Camille beside him and no one to sabotage his way of life, he could forgive old hurts. He wouldn't be able to enjoy the freedom his future held if he didn't.

"As for you," Nathan said, turning to Noah, "I'll pay every medical bill. Camille knows how to get them to me. And I'd like to pay your salary for the time you're unable to work. Bonnie taught me that money isn't the answer. It's the kindness behind it. I know I can't heal what I've done on my own, but I can pray, and I can make sure you're not struggling because of something I did."

The tension in Camille's body eased beside Noah, and he felt the weight she'd been carrying these last few days dissolve.

Noah squeezed her shoulder before releasing her from his hold to lean on his crutch. He might not be able to walk to Nathan without a limp, but he'd face him as well as the Good Lord would allow.

Extending his hand toward the man who'd

stolen years of happiness, Noah vowed to let the hurt go. "Thank you for coming here."

Nathan grasped Noah's hand in a firm shake. "Thank you for letting me see her."

Nathan was right to think that protecting Camille from whatever might come next had crossed Noah's mind. She was his priority—above the land and everything he'd known, and second only to the Lord.

Noah's parents stepped up beside him, and Silas extended his hand to Nathan. "Camille will be safe here. We love her like our own."

Noah's mother nodded. "Yes, she's always been welcome here. We'll take care of her."

Camille didn't approach her stepdad. When Nathan had waited plenty of time for her to decide to come to him in her own time, he raised one hand in farewell.

"It was good to see you, Camille." His shoulders slumped as he returned to his truck.

"Wait," Camille called to him. When she met him at the truck, everyone except Noah stepped back to give them privacy. She'd placed her hand on Noah's crutch in a silent plea for his presence.

"I'm glad you came." Her voice shook, and she stuffed her hands in the back pockets of her jeans. "I know it took a lot for you to come here. I'm just glad this is over. I'd like to move on." Camille lifted one shoulder to her ear. "I just need a little time. I think we all do."

Nathan nodded and his mouth formed a thin line. "Thank you for standing up to me and telling me how wrong I was. I needed that kick, and the one Bonnie gave me too. I needed to get my act together."

Camille released her hold on Noah's crutch and wrapped Nathan in a hug. "I'm happy here. And I do still want to get my law licensing. I want to help people, and I hope you can support that decision."

Nathan pulled away from their embrace. "I do support you. I trust you to make good decisions. At least, I'm learning to step back and let you make them on your own."

He turned to Noah and lifted his chin. "As for you, I know you'll treat her well. I see now that I'll be blessed to have you as a son-in-law."

An apology was one thing, but a blessing had been more than Noah had ever hoped to receive from Nathan Vanderbilt. "Thank you, sir."

Camille twisted the toe of her boot into the dirt. "Maybe we could have lunch sometime?"

Nathan rubbed a hand on Camille's arm. "I'd like that."

Noah and Camille watched Nathan drive away before heading inside. Noah needed to talk to his parents and gauge their perception of the visit.

Voices quieted as they entered the house, and

Aaron and Micah stood from the table in the meeting room.

"Well, is it over?" Micah asked.

Noah nodded. "It's over."

Micah's shoulders slumped in relief, and Aaron let out a heavy breath.

Noah's dad met them with hugs and whispered, "I'm proud of you, son," before moving his attention to Camille.

When his mom stepped up to him, she didn't say anything as she clamped her lips between her teeth and hugged Noah.

He took the moment to whisper, "He gave us his blessing."

Tears pooled in his mother's eyes as she stepped away from him. She was a strong woman, but she carried a tender heart for those she loved.

Micah rested his hand on Camille's back before pulling her into a hug. "Welcome to the family."

Noah hadn't asked her to marry him in so many words yet, but with Nathan's blessing, he had no reason to wait. He could shower the woman he loved with every kindness and adoration, and he'd take full advantage of the freedom in their future.

CHAPTER 34
NOAH

"No, Wayne, I want the office facing west. It can't move."

Noah picked at the edge of the bandages on his leg. He'd spent far too much time lately sitting at the kitchen table in gym shorts with his leg propped in a chair. He got out on the ranch every day, but his hours were much shorter. Plus, he wasn't actually helping. There were few things he could do on his own right now.

Instead, he'd thrown himself into designing a house. He hadn't proposed to Camille yet, but he planned to any day now. Being confined to a sitting position for extra hours had provided the perfect time to build their future—a home.

Noah studied the blueprint and marked the changes the designer suggested. "That might work."

He thought about Camille's house in town. "She'll want to keep the fireplace, though."

A knock sounded at his cabin door, and Noah hastily rolled the blueprints up. "Wayne, I hate to cut you off, but I'll have to call you back." Ending the phone call, he pushed himself up from the chair and grabbed his crutches. "Coming!"

The door opened before he'd gotten a chance to stash the blueprints, so he hastily threw the roll into the corner of the kitchen.

Camille's smiling face greeted him as he tried to mask his unease. She'd been too close to seeing the blueprints, and she would definitely ask questions.

"Hey, there. I'm modifying the tradition due to your delicate state."

Any tension that lingered in Noah's shoulders evaporated at Camille's playful taunts. He was convinced that if she could make jokes about his shredded leg, she must not be too bothered by the injury. In truth, it could have been much worse. He'd been lucky to get by with antibiotics and stitches.

"What tradition?" Noah asked.

"It's your birthday, and I've given you the courtesy of allowing you to sleep in instead of knocking on your window at midnight."

He made his way to her with a smile on his face. "Thank you."

"Plus, you couldn't pay me to sneak around your cabin at night." She shuddered. "No, thank you."

He wrapped an arm around her shoulders and pulled her close. With his crutch still under his arm, the hold was awkward, but he could still kiss her forehead. "No need for sneaking around here when you barely knock."

"Are you saying I should wait on the porch for you to hobble over and let me in?" Camille asked.

"No. You're welcome here any time. What's mine is yours."

"Speaking of what's yours, let's take your truck." Camille jerked her thumb over her shoulder and headed for the door. "It has your present in it."

"Present? You didn't have to get me anything."

Camille rolled her eyes. "Birthday. Presents. It's another tradition."

Noah thought of a gift he'd recently gotten for her. "I'll meet you at the truck. I need to change into jeans."

"Take your time. I'll just hang out with Dixie."

When Camille closed the door, Noah made his way to the bedroom as fast as his crutches would carry him. He did need to change clothes, but he'd really needed some privacy to grab the ring. Shoving it into his pocket, he decided today was as good a day as any.

Dixie bounded back toward Camille with a stick in her mouth as Noah stepped outside.

"You ready?" Camille asked as she met him on the steps.

"I guess so. Where are we going?"

"To the truck first. Your present is waiting."

Noah made his way to the passenger side. He still wasn't comfortable enough with his leg to risk driving, but Camille didn't seem to mind the switch in their roles.

Once he was settled in the cab, she looked at him expectantly. "Well, do you notice anything different?"

Scanning the worn interior, his gaze was drawn to the shiny new radio. "You replaced the radio?"

"I didn't do it by myself, but Nathan helped me this morning. He's handy to have around sometimes."

"That was really nice of him." Noah touched the big round button and adjusted the volume to low.

Camille lifted a shoulder. "He's trying, and that's good enough for me. What do you think?"

"I think it's great. At least I have entertainment options while I'm working now."

Camille gasped and placed her hand on her chest, faking hurt at his words. "I don't entertain you enough?"

"Of course you do, but you're not here all the time. Those days are lonely. Thank you."

She leaned in and kissed him, and he forgot all about the radio and the pain in his leg. Warmth slid down his chest and filled him up. If she said yes today, he could have a lifetime of kisses like this one.

She slowly pulled away and hummed a contented sound. "You ready for the next part of the day?"

Noah sat back in his seat. "Anywhere you want to go, pretty lady."

Camille handled the old truck with ease as they drove to the northern edge of the ranch. As they made their way to Bluestone Creek, he was intensely aware of the ring in his pocket.

"We're here." She held her arms out, indicating the spot they'd claimed as their own. "Happy birthday."

"Best birthday ever." Noah smiled.

"Oh, you're just saying that. I thought we could use any excuse to come out here, especially now that you're out of commission for ranch work."

"Keep making jokes. I might have to take care of you when you're old and broken."

"If I'm lucky," she quipped then hopped from the truck and waited at the front until he righted himself firmly on the ground.

The grass was tall and beginning to die in the changing season, but Camille was patient as they slowly made their way toward the boulder.

Camille tilted her head and brushed a strand of hair from her face as the wind whipped around them. "Okay, maybe I didn't think this through. How are you going to get up there?"

Noah smirked. "I'll make it, but I have something I want to ask you while our feet are still on the ground."

Camille propped her hands on her hips, waiting.

Maybe neither of them had thought this through. How was he going to kneel? "Um, can you use your imagination and pretend like I'm down on one knee?" Noah asked.

Camille's eyebrow rose. "Why?"

Noah pulled the ring from his pocket and offered it to her, but before he could say anything, Camille gasped and her hand flew to cover her mouth.

Her excited gesture clipped his hand and sent the diamond solitaire flying into the creek.

Noah still hadn't fully grasped what had happened when Camille yelled. "The ring!"

"It's okay," he said.

It would be okay. He was going to be certain it would. They just needed to slow down for a moment and figure this out.

"I'll get it!" Camille bounded toward the creek, pulling off her boots.

"Wait! That water is freezing," Noah called out. Inhibited by the crutches, he hoped the urgency in his voice would stop her.

"I don't care. I have to find it." She stepped into the shallow water and sucked in a breath. "Cold. Cold. Cold. Find the ring. Find the ring. Find the ring."

"Camille, please get out of there."

She bent at the waist and stuck her hands into the water. "It landed right around here."

"I'll get you another ring. Just get out of the freezing water!"

Camille twisted to glare at him. "Stop talking. I need to concentrate." Her hands moved beneath the water, digging for the ring.

Noah looked around for anyone to help him convince his impulsive fiancée to get out of the creek, but the closest person was probably a mile away. Was she even his fiancée yet? He hadn't gotten the chance to ask her to marry him, and she hadn't said yes.

"Got it!" Camille yelled, holding up a muddy ring. She quickly dunked it back into the water and swirled it around to wash away the mud. "I told you I'd find it."

She leaned toward him as if she meant to step out of the creek, but her foot stayed buried in the mud, sending her sprawling. Her lower half lay in the water while her arms flailed to break her fall against the bank.

Noah shoved his crutches to the side and limped to her. "How have you managed to fall into the creek twice now?"

"I know," Camille sighed.

"Are you okay? I can't carry you out this time."

"I'm fine." She pushed up onto her elbows before holding up the ring. "Still have it."

Noah shook his head. "I'm not talking about the ring. Are *you* okay? Did you hurt anything? We need to get you dry."

"I'm okay. I'm better than okay." Camille's grin lifted her cheeks as she sloshed out of the water.

Noah released a relieved breath. "Are you able to drive back?"

"I'm wet, not unconscious. Stop fussing."

Camille was beginning to shiver by the time they reached the truck, shaking as she drove to the cabin, and her teeth were chattering by the time they closed the door of Noah's cabin against the autumn wind.

Noah hobbled into his bedroom and grabbed the smallest clothes he owned. They would work until he could get her home. "Here are some clothes. You need to warm up and get dry. Take a shower if you want."

He fought the urge to pace as soon as she closed the bathroom door. Instead, he sat on the couch and propped his leg on the coffee table to wait.

Fifteen minutes later, Camille emerged from the steaming bathroom with wet hair and wearing his baggy clothes. The sight made heat rush to Noah's cheeks as she stretched out her arms and twirled for him.

"Is this a good look for me?" she asked, completely at ease letting him see her in her most raw form.

"Uh huh." Noah nodded.

She jumped onto the couch beside him, and he rested his arm around her shoulders as she snuggled into his side with her feet curled up beneath her.

"You had me worried."

She sucked in a deep breath against his chest. "I'm fine. You were going to ask me to marry you. How could I be anything but over the moon?"

"Speaking of, I never got to actually ask you."

Camille lifted her head and bit her bottom lip to contain a grin. Being this close to her made his head spin every time. She smelled like his soap, and he temporarily forgot what he'd been about to say.

"You gonna do that, cowboy?"

"Do what?" he asked.

"Ask me to grow old with you."

He wasn't sure how much happiness a person was capable of carrying on any given day, but he might have hit the limit.

He lifted her hand and trailed his fingertips over her delicate skin. "Camille, will you let me love you forever?"

"Ye—" He gently placed his fingertips over her lips, silencing her words.

"Wait, let me finish. Will you build a home with me, live a beautiful life of ups and downs with me, raise cattle and babies with me, and let me take care of you when you're old and gray?"

Camille nodded.

Noah asked, "Do you have the ring?"

She pulled it from the pocket of the borrowed sweatpants and handed it to him.

He offered the ring to her and asked, "Camille, will you marry me?"

"Yes," she whispered as a sheen covered her eyes.

Unable to wait any longer, Noah slid the ring onto her finger and sealed his lips against hers. With her body tucked in tight against his, he knew God had given him a gift he'd treasure his entire life. The intensity of their kiss grew as the weight of their decision to become one settled around them.

The kiss drew on, sealing their future in a sweet vow. When it ended, Camille whispered, "There are a million memories I'm grateful to have back, but there is one I'll treasure above all."

"What's that?" Noah asked.

"I'm glad I remembered to love you."

EPILOGUE

LUCAS

Lucas tapped his boots to the beat of "Louisiana Saturday Night." Ansley's hand was warm in his as they danced to their second song of the night. Her tawny hair fell gently over her shoulder, and her smile was as wide as his.

Noah and Camille's engagement party had turned into an all-out celebration once they'd shoved the wooden tables against the walls after supper.

Camille had called it a "casual gathering," but there were easily sixty people milling around the meeting room of the main house.

The song ended, and Lucas turned to Ansley. "I'll catch up to you later." Jerking a thumb over his shoulder, he gestured toward the kitchen. "I need to check on Mom."

He'd known Ansley since they'd started school

together, and the fall of her smile was as expected as the sun rising in the east. They had fun together, but her good mood faded quickly when it was time for them to part ways.

Lucas waved and made his way through the crowd toward the kitchen. Ansley should know by now that he wasn't interested in her romantically, but maybe he should say something. He shook his twitching hand to dispel the nervousness. That was a conversation he'd be happy to save for another day.

A hand grabbed his arm, and Lucas turned to see Camille, eyes bright and smile shining in the twinkling lights she'd made him hang last night.

"Thanks for putting this together. I'm having the best time." Camille wrapped her arms around him and squeezed.

"Sure thing." Lucas got along well with most everyone, but he'd always liked Camille. She hadn't brushed him off as the annoying little brother when she'd been friends with Noah back in grade school.

If the Hardings were getting another set of hands on the ranch, he was glad it was her. She worked hard and had spunk. She also loved the horses, which earned her major brownie points with him.

Camille turned and danced off into the room filled with their family and friends. She and Noah had revealed the plans for their new house tonight, and everyone had gathered around the happy couple with congratulations.

Lucas did intend to check in with his mother, but that wasn't his destination. If Mama didn't need his help, he planned to sneak off to the stables and check on the horses. The cattle, hay, and feed mixing were important, but Lucas was the unofficial caretaker of the horses.

Each of the Hardings cared for the horses, but Lucas's affinity for the spirited animals was the strongest of the family. He'd learned enough from his parents and his grandparents that he could diagnose and treat most ailments without the need to call the local vet.

He liked to think he had a special intuition for the horses. Each one had a unique personality, and he often thought of them as friends.

Dancing was fun, but someone had to keep working when the entire family was celebrating. He needed to talk to his parents about hiring an extra hand to look after the horses, especially since his shift at the fire station kept him away from the ranch for forty-eight hours every week.

Lucas found his mother in the kitchen uncovering another tray of bacon wrapped sausages. "There you are. Need any help?" He leaned against the counter beside her, awaiting instruction.

"No, but thanks. Everything else is taken care of, and Jenny is helping. Where are you off to?"

"Check on the horses." Lucas winked, letting his mom know he didn't mind the chore. "We should check the books and see if there's enough money to hire a horse hand." He grabbed a toothpick-skewered snack from the tray and headed for the back door.

"I agree. Actually, your dad and I already hired someone."

Lucas stopped with the sausage near his open mouth and turned back to his mom. "You did?" Why hadn't they consulted him about this? He'd be the one spending the most time with the new horse caretaker. What if they didn't like each other? He hadn't had a say in hiring Jameson, and Lucas couldn't stand the guy.

His mom lifted her chin and grinned. Her eyes held the promise of mischief. "Don't worry. You're gonna love her."

Lucas didn't hear the door close as Mama left him alone in the kitchen. His heart beat hard and fast in the quiet room.

"Her?"

OTHER BOOKS BY MANDI BLAKE

Blackwater Ranch Series

Complete Contemporary Western Romance Series

Remembering the Cowboy

Charmed by the Cowboy

Mistaking the Cowboy

Protected by the Cowboy

Keeping the Cowboy

Redeeming the Cowboy

Blackwater Ranch Series Box Set 1-3

Blackwater Ranch Series Box Set 4-6

Blackwater Ranch Complete Series Box Set

Wolf Creek Ranch Series

Complete Contemporary Western Romance Series

Truth is a Whisper

Almost Everything

The Only Exception

Better Together

The Other Side

Forever After All

Love in Blackwater Series

Small Town Series

Love in the Storm

Love for a Lifetime

Unfailing Love Series

Complete Small-Town Christian Romance Series

A Thousand Words

Just as I Am

Never Say Goodbye

Living Hope

Beautiful Storm

All the Stars

What if I Loved You

Unfailing Love Series Box Set 1-3

Unfailing Love Series Box Set 4-6

Unfailing Love Complete Series Box Set

Heroes of Freedom Ridge Series

Multi-Author Christmas Series

Rescued by the Hero

Guarded by the Hero

Hope for the Hero

Christmas in Redemption Ridge Series

Multi-Author Christmas Series

Dreaming About Forever

Blushing Brides Series

Multi-Author Series

The Billionaire's Destined Bride

About the Author

Mandi Blake was born and raised in Alabama where she lives with her husband and daughter, but her southern heart loves to travel. Reading has been her favorite hobby for as long as she can remember, but writing is her passion. She loves a good happily ever after in her sweet Christian romance books and loves to see her characters' relationships grow closer to God and each other.

Acknowledgments

Writing hasn't ever been lonely for me. I have so many people in my life who cheer me on daily. My writing friends, Stephanie Martin and Hannah Jo Abbott, push me to tackle my to-do list every day. I have a great beta reading team who don't let me get away with anything. Thank you Pam Humphrey, Jenna Eleam, K. Leah, and Tanya Smith who are the best first readers.

I also want to give a huge thanks to those who shout about my books. Kristen Behrens of Books.-Faith.Love book blog and Kirby of Preppy Book Princess book blog. You've become wonderful friends. I couldn't do anything without my sister, Kenda Goforth. You're a rock star, and I appreciate everything you do.

So much time and effort goes into making a book look pretty in the end. Amanda Walker designed a book cover that had the vision I wanted for this series. As always, I love her work. On the inside, Brandi Aquino of Editing Done Write edited this book relentlessly, and I appreciate her attention to detail.

As always, I owe a great deal to you as a reader. I'm so thankful that you took the time to read this book, and I hope you enjoyed it! I write because I love it, but I also hope *you* love it too!

CHARMED BY THE COWBOY

BLACKWATER RANCH BOOK 2

She's been left before, so now she does the leaving. Can he convince her to stay?

Maddie Faulkner can't seem to find a place to call home, even in her twenties. Getting attached only makes it hurt more when she has to leave. And leaving is inevitable. For now, she's back on the ranch she loved as a child, and desperate to conceal any connection to the crimes of her parents.

Lucas Harding doesn't know what to make of the new horse hand at Blackwater Ranch. She's got walls he can't seem to charm his way past. But they share a love of horses and a deeper connection he can't explain.

The last thing Maddie should do is let down her guard. He'll hate her when he finds out why she left Blackwater Ranch the first time. But when the time comes to say good-bye, her heart might be too attached to leave.

Charmed by the Cowboy is the second book in the Blackwater Ranch series, but the books can be read in any order.

Made in the USA
Coppell, TX
20 June 2024

33742252R00173